To Barbara
May your
Journey
blessed
you read
But A

In But A Moment

She'rri A. Gambrill

Love

10-24-2010

In But A Moment
Copyright © 2002 by She'rri A. Gambrill

For more information, please address the author

Brown Ink Publishing, LLC
P.O. Box 958
Monroeville, PA 15146-0958
www.browninkpublishing.com
Email: dana@browninkpublishing.com

Registered Trademark – Brown Ink Publishing, LLC

ISBN 0-9713092-3-X
Printed in the United States of America

Library of Congress Control Number 2002115595

1. African-American 2. Fiction-General/Contemporary 3. Fiction-Romance

Dedication:

I dedicate this book to the memory of my Beloved Sister/Best Friend, Rhonda Elizabeth Gambrill-West. I am blessed to have had the pleasure of God's wonderful blessing when He blessed me with her as my sister. But most of all, I praise God that Rhonda had a personal relationship with the Lord Jesus Christ and accepted Him as her Lord and Savior prior to her departure. And one day we shall meet again, in the meantime thank you God for my Angel. For through the trials and tribulations I am deemed to face, I feel your smile everyday of my life and the beauty of your wonderful spirit continues to illuminate my life.

Thank yous:

First and foremost I give thanks to my Lord and Savior Jesus Christ for the many gifts He has so graciously bestowed upon me. For it is the Lord I give all Honor and Glory to, for without Him I am **NOTHING**. I am forever grateful for the unconditional love He has poured out upon me and continues to do everyday of my life. Nothing or no one will ever falter my faith in **HIM**!!!

To my Mom, the woman in my life who has molded me into the woman I am today, Delores Gambrill (Dee Dee) thank you for the continued support and unconditional love you have displayed to me. For your prayers and instilling in me that God never changes. Thank you for not only being a wonderful Mother to me, but for being a Best Friend to me as well. But most of all, thank you for believing in me at all times.

My Dad, Clifford Gambrill and Step-mom, Bert Gambrill for your love and support.

My Uncle, Fred Gambrill (Butch) - for your constant support and love you have so unselfishly provided towards me. I will be forever grateful.

III

My Brother Dana N. Gambrill for sharing the gift God blessed you with and sharing the Word of God with me.

My Brother Ryan O'Jaye Gambrill for believing in me and letting me know you are proud of me.

My niece Shana Sha'rre West for listening to my story and feeling it before even reading it. I only pray I will always be the apple of your eye as you are to me.

My Granny, Elese Adams for your many prayers and encouragement and most of all your trust in Jesus!!!

To my extended Family, The Adams, Gambrills and Wards, thank you for who you are and just loving me "for real".

My five best friends, **Bernadette Riles, Diana Mathews, Denise Bailey, Carla Johnson and Wendy Thomas**, who have cried with me, encouraged me and believed in me when others weren't too sure. I'm better than blessed when it comes to "true" friends, I love Y'all.

In the Circle of My Sisters for your many late night talks and encouraging words. Especially to Cordelia Carter for your passing on the right information at just the right time. Thank you!

My former Pastor John T. Davidson, Jr. and church family of Creative Ministries Berachah, Inc. thank you for instilling in me the Word of God and your many forms of encouragement.

My Publishers, Eric L. Brown and his wife Dana Thompson Brown of Brown Ink Publishing, LLC thank you for helping to bring my story to the hearts of those who need it, but especially thank you for having a heart of love for Christ.

Special thank you to all those who took the time to read, listen and encourage, I will always be forever grateful (Mrs. Conswaylo Jefferson, I thank you and love you especially, I still feel your prayers).

Special, special thank you to the one person (you know who you are) who always had my back, believed in me, listened to me, encouraged me and loved me even if it was just for a moment....I am blessed!!!!

*If I have failed to personally name anyone who has helped
me in anyway, please blame my head and not my heart for
you will   always be nestled in the crevasses of my heart
forever!*

<u>**Author's Remarks:**</u>
*Love is the backbone of hope that soars through the wings of
pure joy. Without it we are nothing!!*

Prologue

*For in this life we are equipped with Love, but it is our own
desire to either administrate it or dissolve it, but in one way or
another we will be touched by love. Though in the hearts of
many some have tried to escape it, ignore it, abuse it or even
kill it, but to no avail. For we are here but a moment and
many things can change in the blinking of an eye. But, if you
stare at something too long you'll get lost in the desire of
reaching for it and soon it will invade the privacy of sight and
depict something ugly or something beautiful even your own
eyes can be deceived. Love is but a welcome to the heart and
introduction to the soul. But believing in it goes even further
because it's at that moment one has lived!*

In But A Moment

Shérri A. Gambrill

© **2002**

Jackson Waters and Bill Tilmann are the best of friends. In fact, they're more like brothers. But the love of a woman causes a detrimental hurt between the two. It's a betrayal far beyond hurt that causes a secret identity to be disclosed. In the city of Pittsburgh, Pennsylvania, Five African American Women, along with two African American Men face the challenges of everyday life.

Donna and Nicole Grant are sisters depending on the support from each other as well as from their friends. Donna faces the veracity of genuine love and what it truly means. Then she realizes that there are numerous trials and tribulations associated with it. It takes an outpouring of her spirit to help pull closure to the pain of life's unfair handouts.

Nicole, who is desperate to be in a relationship like that of her older sister's, finds that there's more to love than just having a Man in one's life. She also discovers that love can be found through developing a friendship first. But she wonders if she'll ever find Mr. Right? Her desire of wanting a true relationship and the thrill of playing games soon tarnishes when tragedy happens to her friend. Through it all, true love meets her head on.

Stacie Patterson, the woman with all the right answers, is as compassionate as they come. Her dedication is balanced with equal portions distributed to her job and friends. They depend on her and she is always there for support. Through all of her 35 years, she has observed various forms of violence. In the interim it makes her stronger. And she learns what being in touch with your inner spirit is all about. But the one thing that she longs for the most she cannot have. Or can she?

Michelle Todds, has been longing all of her life for a mother and daughter relationship. After living on the streets at the age of 16, life to her had no real value. Later she finds herself in a position of fighting for the life she felt was not worth living years ago. The terrible lie she tells destroys the one Man who truly loves her. Her mother, who is the only person that can help and heal her pains, turns her back on her. Will her Mother fight with her or will her daughter fight once again alone?

Darletta and Carmella Springer are twins who once loved each other but are now bitter enemies. One becomes revengeful towards the other. And the other begs for her forgiveness. A case of mistaken identity causes one to bear a pain so deep that it destroys the kind heart she once had. The other has such an enormous guilt that she would do anything to mend their relationship. So she agrees to keep the secret shared between them. Will it bring them back together? Or will the secret be told?

In But a Moment everything can and will change!

1

<u>All in a Day</u>

J ackson Anthony Waters struggled to get through the remaining two hours of the day as he stared at the city of Pittsburgh Screen Saver and visualized the past events. Since so much had taken place it was no wonder the headache he tried to escape resurfaced over and over again. Just trying to complete a day's work was truly an impossible task. As he played with the computer keys, he glanced at his gold watch for the umpteenth time hoping the day would end soon. It just seemed as though everything was going wrong.

Even his routine dosage of dealing with his co-worker's constant artificial demeanors was something that he could handle. But today he just had enough. If he could just focus on the last two hours of the day it would finally be over. But with Mr. Woodson's comments put the icing on the cake, he couldn't wait to get out of his office, clear his mind and focus on something pleasant.

Jackson Anthony Waters was a man of character. That's not to say he was conceited mind you, but that he had a great love for his disposition. He was a strong man, not just physically strong, but internally strong. His ambition and his nature to strive for success opened his heart to those he trusted and those whom he empowered in his life. Because he was a self-determined man and spiritually rooted with his oneness, he believed in discovering the good in everyone. But with all his great attributes, Jackson had two difficulties. He had no patience for life's challenges and he was losing patience in waiting to find his queen of a woman.

Jackson was a tall man about 6'3" with a sculpture physique. He had a smooth chocolate complexion, like that of a candy bar and very dark eyes with lashes so long they curled at the end preventing the stroke of his lower lashes.

Jackson's smooth lips made it impossible to not await his smile. But once the display was complete it was worth the wait. His attire was that of the finest and he took great pride in looking good. He had a collection of shoes and suits that out beat any store.

His greatest desire was finding his queen of a woman so that he could share his love and start a family. Through the years he had met plenty of women who fit the description but he just never gave them the opportunity to prove themselves. They were just was no comparison to Carmella Springer, the love of his life, so he thought.

Carmella had all the qualities he was looking for in a woman, he believed she shared the same feelings for him, until Jerome Lockhart entered the scene. Jackson couldn't believe Jerome was able to pull Carmella away from him so easily. Although Carmella cried wholeheartedly when she broke it off with Jackson, he still couldn't believe she would give up so easily. It just didn't make any sense to him.

Jackson gave up rather than feeling like a fool. He figured if she wanted to go he would let her go without a fight. The last thing he needed was someone who really didn't care for or need him. But with a continuing display of the dialog in his mind, his heart grew confused and said otherwise. The decision she made to leave him continued to plague him. There was this woman who he had shared so much with and out of the blue she decides to dismiss their connection with no further discussion. It was almost as if their relationship was just a movie that someone took the remote to and switched the channel.

Happiness was all he wanted for her, even if it didn't include him. Maybe it just wasn't meant to be. He felt in his heart, the woman he was meant to be with would come and complete his world. Still in his heart of hearts he prayed Carmella would come to her senses and come back to him. She had to since he had so much to offer her or any woman for that matter. Now to have to go back out into this iniquitous world was not an easy game plan for him. It would take patience, and again that was one attribute Jackson Waters did not have.

"Hey, hey what's up my brother?" asked a familiar voice.

Jackson continued his walk to the parking garage.

"You headed to the garage?" asked Jackson's friend Bill.

Bill's smile was bright and his voice was enthusiastic as he spoke with his friend. Jackson watched him from the corner of his strained eyes, staying clear of the on coming traffic. Meanwhile his friend glanced at a pretty dark-skinned lady running across the street before the light changed green.

"You know the routine," Jackson stated in a matter of fact fashion. He shook his head to the gesture Bill made as he watched the pretty woman coming towards them. Bill reached in his back pocket and pulled out his sunglasses to escape the sun, which was now blinding his view.

"Man did you see the legs on that lady? She was simply beautiful. With women like that around how could a brother go for a white woman? I never could understand that. Me personally, I've got to have my sister on my arm. Bill shook his head at his own statement as he wiped the tiny beads of perspiration that danced on his forehead.

Jackson continued walking with his long stride ignoring his friend's comments. The last thing he intended to do was chase behind some stuck up woman who was eyeballing his friend. Both men stopped at the corner and eagerly waited for the traffic to diminish before scurrying across the street.

"Awe, come on man, you still messed up over Carmella?"

Jackson shook his head, disclosing a defiant no. "I mean, I've thought of her, but it's not like am loosing my mind over her or anything. If that's what you mean."

The truth of the matter was the fact that he was loosing it. He loved that woman with all his heart. And contrary to his friend's earlier statement, he felt black women were always crying about having a hard time finding a decent black man. Switching his heavy briefcase to his opposite hand, he knew he was a decent black man and had an exuberance of quality just waiting to be released to someone deserving of it. For a split second he could see why black men chose white women.

Black women were never satisfied he thought. If they found a decent black man they still had something to complain about. Being superficial and judgmental was just their nature. They would over-examine a man's speech, his clothes, his job and even his walk. Then they would talk about men being particular not realizing that they had that area perfected. When they have a good man, they don't want him. No, they would rather have some hard, roughneck brother treating them like dirt he thought to himself.

Through it all, he still found black women with all their many hues, beautiful. Because of that he would never turn his back on them no matter how rough they would make it for him. He missed his woman, but he didn't want to appear to his friend as though he was totally distraught about the breakup.

"I was just checking, I know your cool. Hey, how's the job coming? Is old what's his name still tripping?"

"Yeah man. It's hard trying to deal with some folks sometimes. They can get on my last nerve. I mean half of the people in my department feel that I'm undeserving of the position I have now. They felt it should have gone to their white relative. And what's even more asinine to them, is the fact that I'm trying to move beyond this position. I know I'm deserving of it. But you know how it is for a black man in the corporate world. You have to prove yourself 200% in order to get recognized. And that means you have to always work harder than your white associates do." Jackson paused after venting. "It's burning up out here", Jackson said while loosing his tie with one hand and sticking his key in the door of his black sedan.

He slid in and reached over to flip the latch for his friend. Bill slid in and quickly positioned his seat to recline his head in a comfortable position. He breathed a sigh of relief to be out of the hot sun. Jackson started the ignition and clicked on the air conditioner. Then he reached over to push number three on his radio.

"You're listening to the sounds of W.J.A.M.on your radio," the DJ announced in his loquacious manner. "Let me tell you how much of a great time we had at the party last night. If you missed it you don't want to miss tomorrow's. We're sure to be jamming all night long. I'll tell you what, for the next six callers, I have the most demanding party tickets in Pittsburgh, so get on the Jam circuits and call me now."

Both men rode in silence as they reached the parking garage attendant. Bill reached over positioning the digital numbers to 102.7 and the soothing sounds of a familiar tune soothed their ears.

Man, I don't know why you listen to that station any more," Bill echoed to his friend.

"I couldn't listen to it if I wanted to. I can't get it at home or in the office, besides I prefer Jazz anyway.

"I know about 102.7 W.J.A.Z," Jackson said. "I still like W.J.A.M. too.

"Why?"

"I just like it man. I listen to both. Who cares anyway about what station I'm listening to?"

"I'm sure they do", Bill replied moving his head side to side and singing along with his favorite song.

"Excuse me that's one thing I do have a preference on!"

"What?"

"You're crying. Give me a break! Please!" Jackson responded causing both men to burst with laughter.

As Jackson eased his way out of the garage his friend began giving him his normal one on one lecture of working for the white man. Jackson turned the volume up just a little not to fade his friend's voice out completely, but just enough to take the edge off of the annoying conversation that was about to take place.

"See man, I keep telling you to get your own like me. Then you wouldn't have to answer to those prejudice white people. We have got to start doing for ourselves. I mean hey, everybody else except blacks can look out for each other. We're too busy stabbing each other in the back and knocking each other over trying to see who can get to the top first. In the mean time the Koreans are taking over everything," he stated vulgarly. They're bringing their mothers, fathers, cousins, brothers, sisters and their whole country over. But we just sit back and let them," Bill said positioning his body to meet his friend's eyes.

"What? Why are you looking at me?" Jackson asked, while gaining speed to enter onto the Parkway. "I didn't bring them over here."

"Yes, this is true, but we sure do patronize them. I mean, I ain't never seen so many clothing stores and nail salons in my life. And they run them all, of course. We are the people who patronize them. It just really pisses me off," he said shaking his head at his own comment.

"Look man, I had a rough day today at the white man's job," Jackson said with a smirk on his face, knowing he was about to jab his irritate friend. "I really don't want to hear, about me getting my own, at least not right now. "I'm just not in the mood. I mean I agree with what you're saying wholeheartedly, but I'm not in a position of getting my own thing going. I would love to have my own business and I am not saying it will never happen, I just don't foresee it right now in my life."

In But A Moment

"Well man, I feel like if you don't focus on it now, then when is a good time? You need to get yourself into some entrepreneur programs."

"Yeah, okay man," Jackson said, as he clicked on his left turn signal taking exit 9 of the parkway.

His focus wasn't really on the conversation because he kept replaying the day's events in his mind. It was not only a hard day at the job for Jackson, but very straining as well. As far as Jackson knew, the company he was working for was giving him a run for his money by not promoting him. And even though the timing was off, everything that Bill was saying really did make sense. He didn't really have an excuse for not pursuing something on his own now. He certainly had the funds to begin. The more Jackson thought of the way he was being treated, the angrier he got.

First it was Carmella leaving him, now it was dealing with the stress of job politics. There just wasn't any mental space left for it all. He knew he was being discriminated against. After working as a computer administrator for over six years, he had not been promoted. When he applied for the job, he was told if he proved himself, he could be promoted in no time at all. The manager position of the computer administration information unit would be his. He finally figured out that he was just a face to complete a quota. When applying for the position, one of Jackson's major concerns with accepting it was the advancement opportunity. It was stressed to him that those opportunities were very likely and Computer Software Inc. took pride in moving qualified candidates forward as far as advancement. This pleased Jackson and helped to determine his decision to accept the position.

Jackson could still visualize the chalky white fat face of Mr. Woodson. Thinking back, he watched him pressing his cracked pink stained lips to say compliments to him.

"Fine job you're doing Mr. Waters," he said while gently squeezing Jackson's shoulder as he continued his walk

9

to his office. Jackson gave him a half-sided smile and watched him walk back to the office of which he should have had by then. He was the backbone to Mr. Woodson. It was his expertise that made Woodson look good.

Jackson continued to watch Mr. Woodson walk away as the bottom of his pants gathered the dust from the floor, which was appropriate anyway since he always looked as though someone dipped his whole entire wardrobe in a pile of dust. Things were looking up for Mr. Woodson thanks to Mr. Jackson Waters.

"The Foxwell Project was a great success Jackson, your presentation went very well, very well indeed," he said to Jackson as he munched on a stale donut. Mr. Woodson never looked back once he passed Jackson, for if he had he would have seen the vexed look Jackson Waters had all over his face. The more Jackson thought of it the more frustration hung on to stress and created a monster bottled up within Jackson's being. This was the reaction Jackson had become used to receiving and it was beginning to get depressing.

Jackson was usually a very pleasant person and it took an awful lot to get him discouraged. But because of his current stresses, he needed a moment of silence. And even though Bill Tilmann was Jackson's best friend and he loved him dearly he just wasn't in the mood for him.

"So what's on the agenda today, Mr. Clean"? Bill stated interrupting Jackson's thoughts.

"I don't know about you but I am going to the gym to play a little ball. Then I'll call it a night," Jackson said.

Bill and Jackson had grown up together and their friendship remained close ever since. If anyone could get to Jackson on an emotional level it would be Bill. He was in his early 30's had his own landscaping business and always had that fortuitous demeanor, where nothing was going to get him down. He was a very attractive man with small emerald green eyes that gave definition to his strong jaw line. His complexion was an almond color with his dark eyebrows intensifying his already handsome looks.

Whenever Tilmann and Waters got together they almost always got enticing glances from the ladies. Unlike Waters, Tilmann was satisfied with his bachelor status. If he met a woman he liked so be it. Since he enjoyed the way his life was going, it was often that he would express his refusal to settle down. He had his own business, a beautiful home, a nice car and his share of Saturday night dates. But that wasn't to say he never wanted to settle down. Tilmann viewed women as naggers who were in a constant search for a committed relationship or even worse marriage. He couldn't stand someone interrupting his private life. Eventually, he felt the commodity would get old and boring, besides he was doing just fine with the ladies. Though he wished in the back of his mind that he could find someone similar to Carmella, now just wasn't the time. To him she was the epitome of what a real woman was and he felt Jackson was lucky to have found someone like her.

Women like Carmella were very hard to find. Bill believed there weren't many independent women left out there. The few that existed wouldn't allow a man to come anywhere near, or they were in a power mode and claiming that they didn't need a man to feel complete. On the other hand he didn't have patience for women who didn't know what they wanted out of life and he wasn't about to be the ticket for someone to get an all expense paid relationship with him.

He needed to be in control, seeing whomever he wanted to see and not answering to anyone. The only type of woman that would be a match for Bill Tilmann would be someone who was ambition, self-reliant, strong, goal oriented and of course black and beautiful. From his past experiences it was an unlikely episode for his life.

Watching Jackson's face, Bill knew something was laying heavy on his mind. He also knew how much Jackson loved Carmella and how she had hurt him though Jackson would never admit it. He was under the impression that Carmella really loved Jackson, but maybe she fooled them both. Then a sudden desire to discuss the situation with Jackson came to Bill. But after watching Jackson's expression he figured Jackson would come around sooner or later. And Bill knew he would be there for him when he did.

"All right man, after your done playing hoops come by the crib I have something I want to show you," Bill said after they pulled into Jackson's driveway.

"I told you I'm calling it a night after I play ball, so why can't you show me now?"

"Because I don't have it with me right now. Just come by the crib all right?"

"I'll think about it, but I'm not making any promises. It depends on how I feel when I'm done playing."

"Okay, I'll check you out later," Bill exclaimed feeling fine. Then he slapped palms with his best friend and ran across the street.

2
<u>Sister to Sister</u>

"**G**irl, I didn't ask for your smart comments, I just want to know how I look."

"Well it's pretty relevant to me you already know how you look, so why do you need my opinion? For as long as you've been standing in that mirror, what do you need me to say?"

"I can't stand you and you know it," Nicole said as she glanced at her friend from the three-way mirror.

Everything Donna said was true as far as Nicole was concerned. Nicole knew she made heads turn when she walked down the street or even when her presence was known. And that's exactly what she wanted to happen. She worked out faithfully five times a week and was in top shape. She was going to strut her stuff after all that hard work. She wanted men to notice her.

Donna knew the men Nicole dated were not the type of men she would settle down with. For some reason she never felt complete without a man on her arm. But her sister wanted to see her with someone who would treat her the way she deserved to be treated.

Nicole had a caramel complexion with long red shoulder length hair, which happened to be braided for less maintenance. Nicole was a buyer for a major department store located in Pittsburgh, which at times caused her to travel to New York and California. And because she got most of her clothes for free, she always had the latest styles.

Donna who was not only Nicole's best friend in the whole world but she was her only sister. Donna had her older sister's same red hair, except Donna kept her hair cut in the shorter styles. Both women, in their early 30's were very attractive. However, Donna was totally opposite of her older sister, who loved the night scene and its many adventures.

Nicole enjoyed meeting the many gentlemen she found herself entwined with. Every third Friday she and her friends had their once a month rendezvous, which was an opportunity for the women to get together to catch up on the latest adventures of each other's lives. It also created the prefect opportunity to meet Mr. Right.

Donna never participated in the ladies' Friday night adventures. She much preferred to entertain at home. Many times she felt her sister and her friends were too much into game playing. She knew the club scene was a large game and the majority of people who attended these clubs were surely perpetrators of forgery. To Donna, playing these types of games could lead up to people getting hurt. But she figured that's what they expected to happen anyway.

Thinking back, she remembered when she stepped onto the elevator of a office building downtown and there stood an attractive, well-dressed brother. She smiled at him and was just about to speak when he looked her up and down and then focused on the buttons on the elevator wall. Right before the elevator doors were about to close, she saw a nicely manicured hand interrupt the closing machine. Then a very attractive, well-dressed Caucasian woman entered and briefly smiled at Donna while glancing at the black man leaning against the left side of the elevator wall. She slowly removed her purse from her left shoulder and placed it on her right shoulder with the opening snuggled closed to her body. Thoughts of disgust raced through Donna causing her to immediately look back at the guy. He eyed the white woman up and down just as he had with her, the only difference was when he got to her face he smiled and spoke with a flirtatious smile.

"You idiot!" she murmured. "As fine as you are and as well as you're dressed, she still believes you might try and snatch her purse. But no, you don't care as long as it's a white woman smiling back at you."

In But A Moment

Donna slowly rolled her eyes as the elevator continued to ascend. The woman gave an alleged smile and whispered hello in response. The man then proceeded to converse with the woman. Donna stood and internalized the entire disgusting display. She was so agitated she looked at her nails and thought about getting a manicure.

The woman gingerly responded to his questions while glancing upward as a soft bell rang to acknowledge each floor. Donna wanted so badly to ask him what was his problem, but instead she just looked at both of them and got off on her desired floor. Then she concluded that he was probably a cornball anyway.

Donna sometimes felt this particular game playing was another way to put each other down. Why do men have to be so nonchalant with their emotions and attitude she wondered. And why are women so eagerly ready to put their all into a relationship without thinking it through?

"Come on Donna. Hurry up! Stacie and Michelle are due here at 9:00 PM and here it is 8:45 PM and you are still primping."

"Okay, I'm almost ready," Donna yelled as she smacked her lips together and flashing her prefect set of pearly whites smiled back at her.

Donna slipped into her designer black pumps easily as to not disturb her freshly done pedicure. She believed in manicures, pedicures, professional back rubs as well as having her hair done faithfully every two weeks. She took excellent care of herself; she always found time for relaxation and meditation too. She would often tell her sister and friends that they needed to get more into themselves, not in a allure type of way although that was expected, but spiritually. You needed that in your life when the world seemed to be moving to fast and lots of action was going on.

Donna would find time for quiet and peace especially within herself so that she knew who she was and what she wanted out of life. Sometimes her sister and friends could not

15

understand that type of philanthropic gesture. It was okay to be publicly spirited, but sometimes her sister and friends felt she was too good. But Donna knew herself, which made her a better person and made her happy with herself. After all she had to love herself before anyone else could.

There were times when David wanted to act up trying to dilapidate her perfect day. She would always end up telling him to leave especially when she had a positive day. Many a night she would have to end up using her vibrator just for a feel good feeling, and sleep just like a baby. Her vibrator wasn't David by any means but when she got irritated it was the next best thing.

One thing that she really wasn't looking forward to was the Friday night outing she was about to explore. This would be her first since she and David broke up two weeks ago. David didn't try to call her either. He always did let his pride get in the way of his feelings. Well this time she was going to let her pride take over.

David had a real problem with her befriending Oreon. Oreon was a model and a very attractive man so maybe David was just a little jealous. There was no reason to be, because David was just as attractive in his own sort of way. And besides she loved him with all her heart. David refused to get to know Oreon and didn't even want to meet him.

Oreon was gay and Donna had no problem excepting his sexuality. She loved his company and he was a really good person to talk to. What he chose to do with his life was his business. But the way David felt about gay people was another story in itself.

Donna really enjoyed her friendship with Oreon and she wasn't going to let David or anyone else tell her who she could befriend and who she couldn't. Though she missed David very much she couldn't take his jealous rivals any longer.

As she thought about how David had always helped her with her coat, it felt strange doing the ritual herself. Then

16

she walked over to her closet and searched for her matching jacket, a favorite gift from her sister. She slipped into the smooth material and smiled as she played with the zipper. She reminiscence to a time when she and David forgot about a movie they were going to see one evening. He helped her put her coat on and suddenly turned her around to face him. "Have I told you how beautiful I think you are?" he asked as he slowly began to remove her coat as gently as he helped put it on. Donna blushed and watch David 's eyes so intensely because she knew just how much he really loved her. And at that very moment she also knew that she wanted him more than anything in the world.

He watched her closely as the sun painted a duplicate silhouette of her on the wall. Then she touched his face and interrupted his thoughts of her.

"We better go, the movie starts in 30 minutes."

3
<u>Slow Motion</u>

Softly a voice whispered on the phone as Stacie Patterson held the receiver under her chin. "Stacie are you ready?"

"Yes. Are you coming now Chelle?"

"Yeah, I just wanted to make sure you were ready, cause you know how you are," Michelle stated with a smile.

"Well for your information I was waiting on you," Stacie said while fumbling for her shoes.

"Yeah right. That's why you took so long to answer the phone."

"Just come on," Stacie said to her friend. Then she replaced the receiver and began to search for her other shoe. She really didn't want to go to the club but she knew it was something everyone looked forward to and she didn't want to spoil the fun.

Stacie was the oldest of her three friends who looked up to her and valued her opinion. To them, Stacie was the one who always had it together so they confided in her on topics that were not of knowledge for the others. She wore conservative attire and often times that same attire was spilled over into her nights out on the town. Her friends would sometimes tease her, especially Michele.

"Girl you look like you're about to interview the brothers. Why don't you loosen up?"

"That's right! I am going to do some interviewing. I've got to see what I'm getting myself into, and I don't want him looking at my body first without seeing my mind. Unlike you, trying to catch their attention with those peanuts your trying to camouflage. I wonder what you stuffed in it," Stacie stated rolling her eyes at her friend while the other ladies laughed in perfect harmony. "And why don't you tighten up? I think you're a little to loose Miss Thang."

In But A Moment

While Stacie was intelligent, pretty and fun to be around, she was a strong independent woman who demanded respect and usually got it. Her parents died during a robbery on Hamilton Avenue ten years ago. After her parents' death she and her brother Stan, went to live with her grandmother. But through it all they both turned into productive achievers and hard workers. Stan moved to Los Angeles and landed a job with a prestigious law firm. Later, he married and had two sons. Stacie graduated high school and continued her education at the Pittsburgh University where she earned her Business Degree and later her Masters. She landed a job at Special Partnerships where she became the director of Children and Youth Services.

Stacie knew that she was going to play an active role in the lives of children, but sadly after a diagnosis that demanded a hysterectomy she also knew she would never bear her own. Her condition saddened her for a while causing severe bouts of depression. And though she would speak to few about the situation, she would often wonder if she would find a man to love her regardless.

Mrs. Huggins who was a very good friend to her mother and father and who was a like a second mother, was one of the few that Stacie would share her problems. Her real name was Manza Clara Huggins. But Stacie called her Manzi.

"I will never be able to be a mother," she began to cry. "I always hoped in my heart to be surrounded by children and that I would one day be a mother, Manzi. I don't understand. I just don't feel like a complete woman." She could feel the burning sensation deep in the pit of her stomach. "The purpose God made women is for them to bear children. I'm so shamed." She tried to gulp at the tension caught deep in her throat. "I'm sorry," she told her mentor as she wiped away the tears. But as fast as she wiped them away the more they poured.

She watched the woman as she held her and cried in her bosom. Her eyes focused on the smooth complexion of her face and the powerful yet gentle eyes that looked back at her. It was impossible to tell that she had already lived for 75 years. She was a strong woman with great wisdom. Her spirituality announced itself at the very moment one looked into her eyes. She never lied to Stacie and she knew the look she was receiving was the look of truth. She had a motherly love and disposition about her that made anyone feel safe and comfortable in her presence.

Her hands were strong and ageless. The strength of wisdom was defined in the depths of the tiny lines disclosed in those hands. And the slender long fingers only made the extension of her reach more achievable. She delivered many messages just in her hands alone, for her gestures were never misconstrued. Manza was a woman of distinction and Stacie valued whatever her opinion was.

"Baby listen to me," Manza said slowly while holding Stacie's face and looking into her light brown eyes. "There's more to being a woman than just bearing children, honey."

She felt Stacie's pain and was sure that God would not leave her. Looking far into her eyes she felt as though she could touch her soul. So silently she prayed that God would give her the right words to say to Stacie. In her soul and her spirit she knew that Stacie was going to be blessed if she could just trust and believe in God and let him take care of it.

As a healing power flowed through her hands, she touched Stacie's face. Manza did not know how dedicated, strong and powerful her hands were. They were tools of pure dedication that were always prepared to do the job.

"You think every woman who bears children makes her a woman? Not at all honey. I know plenty of women who have had many children and could care less about being a mother. For it's not the bearing of a child that makes a woman or a mother." She watched the tears well up again in Stacie's eyes. It touched her heart for she could feel the pain she was carrying within. "You can be a mother without doing the actual act of bearing children. This is what makes a real woman. Remember what I'm telling you okay?"

Stacie watched and listened as Manza began to speak.

"Honey a real woman is a virtual woman, one who has goodness, integrity, uprightness, justice, morality, prudence and wisdom, and yes she can be a mother too. Even if it's not her own child. Yes, my baby it's beautiful to be able to bear children, but if that is not in God's plan for you to do that, it doesn't make you any less than a woman. God is going to bless you Stacie, you will be surrounded with children, I see that."

She looked away from Stacie and focused on the tiny bracelet around Stacie's wrist. "What's this?"

"Oh this is a bracelet my mother always wore. She loved birds so she collected them. It was something my Dad had given to her."

"Why are there only two birds on the bracelet? I knew that she collected birds. In fact I had given her some. But I don't think I remember seeing your mother wearing this," she said gingerly lifting the tiny bracelet from Stacie's wrist again.

"That's because my dad gave it to her on the night they ah…." She felt the tears beginning to form again. "I'm sorry. My dad…." Unable to finish her story, she wiped her face with the back of her hand. But wiping her tears with her hand did not stop the tears from flowing. Manza reached up and held her face with her hands. Suddenly the tears began to cease.

"It's okay honey." Manza knew it was hurting her to talk about it, but she felt there was a message there and she needed to hear what Stacie was trying to say. "Your dad gave this to your mother? When Stacie?"

"He gave it to her the night they were killed." She grabbed onto the bracelet as her remaining tears landed on the birds.

"I know it's hard to talk about it, but why are there only two birds?" she asked feelings as though something was about to be revealed. "Your daddy knew that your mother loved birds too. It's odd that he would only place two birds on the bracelet and not a whole flock."

"Dad said she was as beautiful as a sparrow, so he placed a sparrow on it." Stacie suddenly remembered how they shared things so the thought saddened her a little. She only hoped and prayed she would fall in love with a man like her father. "He also said she gave him peace so he placed a dove on it too," she continued.

Manza knew that was the message that needed to be revealed and she thanked God for allowing her to see what it was. She smiled at Stacie as they sat quietly in the tiny kitchen. Then she leaned to the side and grinned as she felt the presence of her friend.

"Oh baby come here," she said rocking her in her arms. "You remember what I've told you honey. You're someone special and no one can take away your mother and father." She placed her hand over Stacie's heart, and she could feel the rapid beat. "You remember you're a great woman in every way."

Stacie often wondered how many people could say they love their occupation. She really loved her work and enjoyed going to work everyday. Her job was both rewarding and challenging, and she helped to create a new beginning for a child. Yes, Stacie worked long hours at times, but if long hours helped in saving the life of a child, it was surely worth it.

Shortly she heard the car horn of Michelle's Honda tooting away. Michelle insisted that Stacie drive. One reason was, she knew if Stacie would take her car she could try to ease her way out early.

Michelle was a very good friend to Stacie, but they were totally opposite. Michelle was very laid back with not a care in the world. Sometimes that was detrimental for Michelle. She was an only child, and there were constant bitterness between Michelle and her mother. Michelle's mother totally disrespected her, and put her down constantly which in turn caused Michelle to have a very low self-esteem. Michelle moved out of her mother's house at the age of sixteen. She was very street smart after two years of living on the street. It's hard for Michelle not to listen to the smooth talking brothers out there who were paying her some attention. The first smooth talking brother that came her way she was on him. Michelle needed to hear the words "I love you" because she never heard that growing up. She was just very naive when it came to men. She trusted them with her life.

When Dennis Gordon came into Michelle's life, she thought he was the best thing in the world. To her, he made her world complete, and at first, Stacie believed Dennis really cared about Michelle. In time, however, Michelle began to complain to Stacie more often than less. She thought that Dennis was cheating on her. But she didn't have confirmation of it. Michelle loved Dennis so much she didn't want to believe it he was cheating on her, so Michelle ignored her suspensions.

Michelle and Stacie met at work. Michelle worked as a word processor and slowly but surely they got to know each other and became really good friends. At first, Michelle didn't care for Stacie. She felt that Stacie thought she was better than the average sister because Michelle had a good job that paid big bucks. Michelle thought Stacie had a somewhat snobbish attitude, but Michelle was pre-judging. Stacie was a sweetheart after Michelle got to know her. At times Stacie had the tendency to pour her professionalism on too heavy. That was just her way. It wasn't because she was trying to act better than anyone. She was headstrong at times and usually tried to motivate whoever was in her presence. Once the exterior melted down, Stacie was funny, laid back and ready to cut up.

Stacie approached Michelle and introduced herself. After all there were not many African-Americans working for the corporation especially on her floor. Stacie wanted to get to know another African-American as soon as she spotted one. There was something about Michelle that intrigued her. She felt somewhat lonely for Michelle. She wanted to get to know Michelle and try to encourage her because she saw signs of depression in Michelle.

Although Michelle was very good with computers, she wanted to try to motivate her to move forward and enhance her skills for better opportunities. Stacie was a go-getter, and she thought everyone else had that same type of mentality. Stacie often shared encouraging words with Michelle to help get her back on track. Michelle was going to enroll at the University next year. Because she loved working with computers and numbers, Stacie encouraged Michelle to go back to school and get a Bachelor's degree in Computer Science. She was excited about starting school.

Since Michelle didn't have much family, she secretly adopted Stacie as her sister. Stacie encouraged Michelle in many ways. When Dennis admitted he was cheating on Michelle and broke her heart, Stacie was right there helping her get through it.

Michelle had done well too until she and Stacie went to the mall and saw Dennis with his new woman. When Michelle saw that the woman was white, she hated Dennis and white women from that point forward. It surprised Stacie especially since Michelle herself looked biracial. Although she often wondered about Michelle's ethnic background, Stacie never brought it up. Michelle was a very intelligent, attractive woman, but she never thought it. She was always putting herself down. Michelle never thought she was good enough, or capable of accomplishing things. That's why it was so important for Stacie to find encouraging words to say to her. Although they would joke quit often, there were so many things that indicated Michelle was having difficulties, especially with white people.

Dennis tried to be cordial to Michelle by saying hello to her at the mall, but she wasn't having it. "Don't you ever part your lips to say hello to me again in life," she said as she walked up to him. "You left me for this white tramp."

Michelle knew she didn't have to go there. She was so angry and hurt she could feel the tears burning in her eyes as she prayed silently for God not to let them drop.

"Now Michelle that's not necessary. You don't have to go calling her out of her name. She ain't no tramp, so stop making a scene and making a fool out of yourself, girl."

Dennis moved closer to Arlene. He knew just how angry Michelle was, and he knew when her temper set in there was no telling what she might do.

"I know you ain't trying to defend that whore, you sell out!" Michelle screamed in both their faces while tears escaped and rolled down her face. Stacie pulled her arm and told Michelle to come on because it was not worth it.

The white girl turned her back and began walking away from the scene. Dennis ran towards her to comfort and protect her. It kind of made Stacie mad too because she knew how much it hurt Michelle to see her man was cheating on her with a white girl. There was nothing worse than a black man dumping a black woman for a white woman was.

Michelle was so upset they ended up going home and not shopping. Stacie comforted her friend and got her through it. Ever since that episode with Dennis and his new girlfriend, Michelle had a hard time dealing with black men and white women. Stacie understood what Michelle was feeling because it would bother her too, but there was something more with Michelle. Stacie could not really put her finger on it.

Stacie was really starting to believe that Michelle was biracial. Michelle did so much to overcompensate for her light complexion. She was always going to tanning salons to make her skin look darker. She even bought make-up a shade darker than her normal color. Michelle was hurting inside, and Stacie was determined to help her anyway she could.

Stacie had a couple of white girlfriends, but she some how would never trust them completely and she felt bad about that. For they treated her good. But she also knew she couldn't go to their neighborhood without the glares and wonders of how a black woman was able to drive a luxury car and pull up in a white neighborhood.

One day, as Stacie got out of the car, she heard a remark from a white woman made to her daughter. So she proceeded to walk up the driveway of Sarah Verbil's home.

"I like your car", the little white girl said, walking towards Stacie's car.

"Oh, well thank you. That's a pretty spiffy bike you have there too," Stacie said smiling at the little girl.

Without any warning, the fragile woman pulled the little girl along. "Honey come on, that's not the lady's car, that's her company car."

The comment stung at Stacie's face and she had to respond. "Excuse Miss. Miss?"

The woman continued to walk ahead as the little blond girl looked back at Stacie.

Stacie caught up with the woman and prepared her words. "No it's not the company car. I worked hard for that car and I'm proud of that. Oh and by the way, I have the say so on who gets a company car or not. I am also the boss. Thank you." In saying that, she turned, smiled and continued her walk to Sarah's house. The little girl placed her hand to her mouth and giggled.

"Excuse me!" yelled the woman as Stacie savored victory.

Stacie stopped and turned to face the woman. She was thinking that there was no way the woman would go there.

"I'm not sure what you call a boss to be. I'm sure you're not doing anything but taking care of the secretarial pool. It always amazed me how a group called Affirmative Action could actually place people of color into position. That's only because they can't get the position on their own." The woman was bitter towards black people, and she didn't like them coming into her neighborhood. "You know how you people are, if you're not waiting for an hand-out, you have boyfriends who sell drugs and you call that a business. I never could understand how you woman could tolerate that." She spun on her heals and started to walk away.

"No, I don't have a drug selling boyfriend. And yes, you're right about Affirmative Action. It's because of people like you that talented, intelligent blacks are not treated fairly in the corporate world. And no, I'm not head of the secretarial pool. Wait! I don't have to explain anything to you. Maybe you need to get out there and get your own job!" she said moving closer to the woman. She could feel the burning sensation deep within her about to surface.

"Oh but I have a job, I'm raising my daughter, that's a job in itself. Of course maybe you wouldn't know that since you all have so many without being married and you use it as an excuse for not getting a job. My husband does support us." The comment hit Stacie where she had never been hit. Stacie walked right up to her face as close as she possibly could and looked her directly in her eyes. She knew the woman was very prejudice and could not control her tongue. So she turned her face and slapped her as hard as she could.

"Oh you better be careful, there may be a chance your face could turn black. After all I did touch you." And with that she walked away leaving the woman wiping her cheek so hard Stacie thought she was going to puncture herself.

Stacie laughed as she continued her walk. She knew Miss Thang wouldn't have anything smart to say back after that.

She really had a good laugh when she told Susan what had just happened. Susan told her the woman was George Nicholls' wife. George worked in the computer center as a supervisor. She couldn't wait until he got home to dinner. George often met with Stacie concerning computer enhancements for her folks. She was going to make a point to let him know. After all he often claimed to have so many black friends.

Michelle on the other hand had an opinion of white women now that no one could change and she placed them all in the same category. Michelle felt white women were always after black men and that disturbed her. She just never thought it would happen to her. Especially when Dennis would always have something derogatory to say when he saw a black man and white woman together. Or was he just doing it for her benefit?

After that scenario Michelle would no longer trust men. She was really out to get what she could from men. She made a promise to herself and to Stacie that she would never give a man her heart again. If there was going to be any game playing she was going to be the one doing it.

Stacie wondered about Michelle quite often because she knew when she said something, she meant it and would carry it out to the limit. She just hoped she didn't get hurt playing her own game.

Michelle mumbled to herself while waiting for Stacie. "She has got to be the slowest girl in history. She'll probably be late for her own funeral." Just when she thought it, Stacie ran out the door.

"Okay let's kick it girl!"

"Yeah, right like you been ready," Michelle said with a sigh. Stacie ignored her comment and pulled the overhead flap down to put on her lipstick.

"You really look nice. That dress is sharp! Is it new?" Michelle asked. "I can't believe you are finally wearing something a little sexy for our night on the town. You know how you go. I'm sure you got a double-breasted suit jacket stuffed in your purse to throw on when we get out of the car."

"No, for your information I felt a little sexy tonight. Don't ask me why. It's been so long since I felt like being a little sexy I didn't think I remembered how."

"Well from what I can see, you really do know how to get sexy every once in awhile. You go girl!" Michelle said as she looked at her friend from head to toe. Stacie smiled at her gesture and flipped the overhead flap back in its original position.

"Oh to answer your question, this dress isn't new. I just never wore it," Stacie said while smoothing out the bottom.

"Girl, you the only person I know that got so many clothes you forget what you got. Of course I only thought you had gear for work. You sure did shock me tonight coming out looking like Miss Thang." They both laughed.

"I'm going to ignore that comment okay? Cause you know I could say something, but I'm not even going to go there," Stacie said viewing Michelle as if something was out of place on her.

"Like what? Is there something wrong with my outfit?"

"No, you look fine. Just drive," Stacie stated motioning her hand to move forward.

Michelle smiled at her friend and shook her head and put the car in drive and moved forward. "So are you ready for a fantasy evening with all the bull included?" Michelle stated while waving her hand for added emphasis.

"If you know its bull, why do you always want to go?" Stacie asked.

"Cause girl, am just playing the game."

"Well, I would think the game would be pretty tired by now. I mean after all, we're not getting any younger, right?"

"Well, as I recall you all have about five years on me. So I guess you would call that old," Michelle said laughing.

"For me, I really don't think Mr. Right is out there. It's all about playing games, therefore I may as well play along and enjoy the ride."

"Well you better make sure the ride has a destination or you better get off at the next stop," Stacie told her.

"That's just it. I don't care if it has a destination or not. I'm just here for the ride and that's it."

29

"Oh, okay, well ride on my sister! Go ahead and miss out on a chance of enjoying that ride of knowing exactly where you're headed."

"Oh girl please! You're so serious. Loosen up."

"No, you better tighten up and take life a little more seriously. You never know when your ride is up for real," Stacie told her friend.

4
Special Guest

B ill tossed the ME magazine onto the small glass table directly in front of the sofa when he heard the front door bell. "Finally," he whispered, satisfied his friend had finally shown up. While making his way to the front door, he yelled out to his friend. "It's about time! I was about to call it a night."

"I hope not," a soft voice replied as Bill swung open the door, to see a timid and fragile Carmella standing before him.

"Carmella what are you doing here?"

"Bill I know it's late but I really need to talk to you. Please don't tell Jackson I was here. He can't know about our conversation at least not yet, okay? Please promise me that."

"Okay, but that may be difficult since he is due to come by here any minute."

"Well, he can't know I've been here," she said with a slightly irritated tone.

"Why not Carmella? What the hell is going on with you? Why did you break it off with Jackson anyway?" Bill knew he was beginning to sound argumentative but he wanted an explanation for Carmella's visit. Why would Carmella come to him? Was she afraid to confront Jackson because it was to soon? Was she in some kind of trouble with that Jerome character?

He observed her very closely. She didn't appear to him like she was in any kind of harm or danger. She was so pretty he thought to himself, a very petite woman with jet black eyes and hair to match. Carmella had the prettiest darkest complexion. She truly was a black beauty with a beautiful smile that always brightened her face eminently. But he noticed that she was very apprehensive.

"Come in," he stated as he opened the door. She

thanked him while trying to preserve her disposition.

"Would you like something to drink?" Bill asked in a delicate tone as to not interrupt her emotional state.

"No thank you. I would just like to get to the point of the matter."

"Okay fine," Bill stated while watching the woman who had made his friend's life so happy and complete. Just as she was about to begin, the phone rang and nearly made her jump to the ceiling. "Calm down girl, it's just the phone, excuse me for one minute," he said while reaching for the phone but never letting his eyes leave the woman. "Hello?"

"Hey man it's me, I don't think I am going to come over tonight. I played ball a little longer than I anticipated and I have to admit that my bones are not as young as they use to be. I am feeling it now," Jackson exclaimed with a chuckle.

Bill did not answer. Instead he was so preoccupied with Carmella for a minute he didn't hear what Jackson had just said. He let the receiver dangle from his hand.

"Bill are you there man?"

"Oh yeah, man, I'm here. Okay I'll check you out tomorrow then."

"Oh I get it," Jackson said with a partly removed voice. "You have company and you were hoping I wasn't coming. You're a trip man. Because I'm so tired right about now I'll let you slide for now."

"You know me so well man. I'll check you out tomorrow then," Bill said trying to sound convincing.

"Okay, later man."

"I guess that was Jackson?" Carmella asked.

"Yeah," Bill said wondering what the evening was all about. "All right, Carmella what is this all about?"

The curious woman watched Bill, searching his eyes and hoping he'd fall right into the game she was about to begin. She began to twist the string of her jacket until it began to knot. Bill walked over to where she sat and placed his hands over hers. Slowly he began to speak.

32

In But A Moment

"Carmella, please what is going on with you? Just say what you came to say. Nothing could be that bad. Come on, obviously, you came to me for help. And I am going to try and help you if you let me."

A slow smile surfaced over her smooth face and her big dark eyes displayed a sparkle of hope. "Sucker!" she smirked. She knew from the heighten concern he displayed that Bill would be easy prey. Thoughts began to filter through her mind. "Maybe he is right I am making too much out of the situation. I have got to do this so I may as well begin with Bill. He looks like a guy who would keep his word, so I guess I am just going to have to trust him. Hopefully he won't mention this conversation to Jackson until I have the opportunity to sort things out. Jackson, now he's another story! He is going to go completely off when he finds out. And if Bill doesn't freak first I'll be able to tell Jackson too. Bill will calm down much faster than Jackson therefore I'll have a better chance with Bill than Jackson at least for now. But one way or another Jackson Waters is going to find out and when he does, he is not going to be pleased." Silently she prayed that she was doing the right thing.

"That Bill is really something. He's always got a date," Jackson thought after hanging up the phone. He hoped that Bill would settle down one day soon. He dated a lot of beautiful, intelligent women from what he could see. Many times his dates got in touch with him to ask for his advance about Bill. Jackson always ended up telling Bill when one of his ladies would call him for advice regarding him. Bill would just shrug it off. Jackson knew Bill treated his women very well. He also knew how women claimed it was so hard to find confident, hardworking, intelligent and attractive men. So he knew if a woman got her hands on Bill they tried to cling on to him for dear life. Like himself, Bill was a great catch.

"Maybe this one was a winner," he said walking to the bathroom and clicking on the shower.

He stepped out of his sweat suit and climbed into the hot vibrating water. He began to reminisce about the shower days he and Carmella had. Those days seemed like just yesterday, he thought while lathering up with soap. No sooner he let the hot water hit his body he'd hear the soft sweet voice of Carmella.

The strong ripple of his body only enticed her even more. She watched as the tiny beads of water absorbed his strong muscular body. She caressed his body with her eyes and touched him with her mind. Observing him that way began to make her heart race to the sound of the water.

5
Be Still My Heart

"Hey Donna, they're here," Nicole shouted from the living room. "Come on girl."

"Okay I'm coming just let me grab my purse," Donna shouted back while rushing to the bedroom.

"Hey girl what's up? You look fabulous," Stacie and Michelle stated in unity.

"Y'all are looking good too," Nicole replied while sliding into the car to make room for her sister.

"Hey where's Donna?" Michelle asked while taking a second look in the rearview mirror.

"Oh she's coming. You know how slow she is."

"Yeah it seems like she and your girl here should have been sisters," Michelle said looking at Stacie and smiling.

"Good thing she isn't my sister. Because if she was we wouldn't be with y'all."

"And why not?" Nicole asked with an irritated tone.

"Because if she was my sister we would be with two fine brothers cruising the islands instead of sitting in this car headed to the club."

"No, if she was your sister you would be pissed off because her slow behind would have y'all missing the boat!" Nicole laughed.

"Well in that case they'd both be missing the boat, cause Stacie wouldn't be to far behind Donna running for it. They both slow as hell," Michelle stated.

"But you forgot I said we'd be with two fine brothers! And believe you me they ain't gonna get on that boat without us!" Stacie added.

"Yeah right, you keep thinking that. They'll be waving to you and Donna from the dock with some other fine women who happen to be on time and dateless," Nicole said smacking Stacie on the back of her head.

"Girl you are so crazy," Michelle said laughing.

"Aha! Laugh on my sisters! Y'all fit right into that category of being deranged."

"All Stacie we still love you girl," Michelle told her.

"Y'all do? Since when?" Stacie shouted in her most mysterious voice while looking at both women like she was serious.

Donna slammed the front door and walked to the car, just in time for the ladies to chew her out for being so slow.

"Well it's about time, slow behind number two," Michelle screamed out the window.

"Oh hush up girl! Let's just get this night over with," Donna said while stepping into the car.

"Now girl you know what they say. When you really don't want to go some place that's when you have the most fun. Cheer up Donna you might meet Mr. Right tonight."

"I had Mr. Right, thank you very much!"

"Who David Johnson?" Michelle asked while watching her friend through the rearview mirror.

"Yes, I do mean David Johnson."

"Girl, please! Get over it. Forget him. It's obvious he wasn't too right or y'all wouldn't have broke up over something so juvenile."

"Oh, Michelle, please. Don't worry Donna he'll be back. Ain't' no body out there gonna give that man what you have. Or should I say, give it to him like you did. And get your minds out the gutter. I wasn't speaking about sex either. I mean Donna," she began looking at her friend. "Can't nobody make David feel complete the way you can. The both of you had that special connection. There's nobody out there who can give him that connection again," Stacie stated turning completely around in her seat to look her friend straight in the face.

Donna smiled and could feel herself beginning to cheer up a little. Her friends always did that to her. They were like therapeutic telepathy. She knew they loved her even though they teased each other often. She knew in her heart that they didn't want to see her hurt or down.

"He's probably home thinking about you right now," Stacie said interrupting Donna's thoughts.

"Or thinking about what lie he can tell to get you back," Michelle said sucking her teeth. "Girl, they're all dogs, every last one of them. They're just out to see what they can get and who they get to satisfy them. Then they leave you hanging. Even the ugly ones got the nerve to try and run a game. Girl let him go! It took but a minute for him to move on. Look at it like this. As quick as it took him to get over you, you can do the same just that fast. Tonight is your night, doll," Michelle said popping her finger in the air. "You're a beautiful sister and you were good for him, but see they don't want the beautiful, decent, classy, lady type. No, they dog them big time. They rather have the little sleazy type women. They don't want no one decent, cause they wouldn't no how to treat them. All they want to say is she thinks she's too good. Oh and Girl, don't let the sister have a decent job, then their really intimidated. They say they want a challenge, but when they get it, they're ready to give up. Naw, my sister they don't want a woman who has herself together. Oh no, oh n…."

"Michelle, shut up already!" Stacie said. "Girl you sound like you're the spokesperson for 'give up on all men'. Chill out," Stacie told her and turned her attention to Donna.

"Don't listen to her Donna. She ain't had no loving in so long she done gone vacuous. David will come around. Give him time. He'll be back you'll see. But for tonight enjoy yourself. Okay?" Stacie concluded.

"Yeah girl chill out. Cause I'm gonna have a ball. Follow your big sister, sweetie," Nicole said, attempting to cheer her sister up anyway she could.

"No thanks," Donna said looking at her sister through glassy eyes.

"Party over here! Party over here!" Nicole shouted. Michelle joined in as Stacie and Donna both looked at the women and shook their heads. Donna sat back in the seat and thought what a night it was going to be.

Nicole hoped silently that her sister would have a great time. She didn't want her to be down and out over a man. She was a little jealous of David and Donna's relationship. Hell, sometimes she wondered if they were really in a serious relationship. They seem to have so much fun with one another, and Nicole knew that Donna shared many things with David. Sometimes she wondered if she shared a little too much with him and did not give her that same consideration when it came to confining in her.

One thing she did know about Donna was that she really loved David. Donna was a strong person and Nicole wished that she was a little more like her. But she was so use to just having a date, she didn't think about a long-term relationship. She knew many of the men she dated used her as a trophy and when they got tired they moved on. Looking at Donna and David inspired her a little. She wanted a lasting relationship. Secretly she was tired and wanted someone to build her life with. She wanted a committed relationship with someone she knew deep down really loved her.

Donna was always talking about love. She really believed in love and thrived on it. Donna spent a lot of time with David, but always continued to make time for herself as well as her friend Carmella Springer. She and Donna became good friends after Carmella landed the cover page of an airline magazine.

Donna and Nicole really liked Carmella because she was a nice and quiet pretty girl. Though, neither woman would consider the same for Carmella's twin sister Darletta, who Nicole and Donna both despised. Carmella was an airline stewardess and because of her travel, she was never around. Her sister, Darletta was a model for Exclusive Touch Modeling Inc.

In But A Moment

Darletta, was very self centered, devious and ruthless. Both women had very distinct looks and were extremely pretty. Carmella paid no attention to her looks, but her sister thrived on hers. Nicole and Donna knew Darletta was severely jealous of her own sister. She wanted to have all the attention and loved the idea that Carmella was timid, because she could walk all over her. But, she would always say how much she loved her sister and how she would do anything for her. It was a corrupted type of love Nicole felt. Because they were twins she would say that she knew when Carmella was hurting. Carmella was a down to earth type person, where Darletta could be a real witch. Through it all Carmella would do anything for her twin and she usually did. It was almost as if she felt she owed her sister something. But Nicole felt the more Darletta was away from Carmella the better.

Carmella hooked up with Jackson Waters and neither Donna or Nicole met him. Carmella was basically with him and they knew she really loved him. Nicole made a mental note to ask Donna about Carmella.

"Okay, ladies put on your best performance," Michelle announced after parking the car in front of the club. Nicole unfastened her seat belt and left the thoughts of Carmella and Darletta in the car.

"Yes, I am ready," Nicole said while holding the seat for her sister. "Let's get it," she shouted walking to the club.

"Ten dollars ladies," said a dark skinned.

"Dang! Ten dollars? I better come out with two fine brothers," Michelle stated slapping the bill in the man's hand.

"Dang!" Donna softly moaned.

"What's wrong girl?" Nicole asked looking at her sister.

Donna pointed to a small table across the room. "There's David and he's here with a woman."

6
<u>Mask</u>

W ell, Bill I really don't know where to begin, but I have to get this off my chest was what ran through her mind. She opened her mouth while trying to select just the right words to say.

"Well I suggest you start at the beginning," he said beginning to get frustrated with her.

"Well I guess I'll just come out and say it then. I'm gay, Bill. And Denise and I are lovers. We've been living together ever since Jackson and I broke up. Jerome Lockhart is my first cousin and I got him to play along with the game. I am so sorry to have hurt both you and Jackson, but I have to be my own person. And being gay is part of my being. People are going to have to accept me as I am because I am happy. There I said it," she stated trying to catch her breath while looking down at her hands because she was so afraid to look Bill in the face.

"What girl, slow down you have got to be tripping!"

"No I am not tripping it's the truth."

"Well I'll be! As fine as you are girl, you didn't even have to go there. Dang!" Bill stated getting up from the couch and walking over to the large African picture hanging over the mantel. "Well how long have you been this way?" he asked with a confused look on his face.

"Bill excuse me but it's not something I just picked up one day. I have always been gay. I was just too busy trying to please everyone else. I didn't think of how I truly felt and what was really going to make me happy."

"Well why couldn't you have been honest with Jackson? And why were you with him anyway? From what he told me, you weren't acting gay in the making love department girl. Dang!" he grimaced.

"I know this is pretty heavy stuff," she stated.

"Yeah you're darn straight girl," he told her.

"I didn't tell Jackson because like I said I was trying to hide it from myself. I was caught trying to be someone I wasn't. I thought that if I could have a relationship with Jackson then I had to be okay. So I faked a lot of things with him. But I was not happy with him. The last thing I wanted to do was hurt him."

"Well why are you telling me this now, after you and Jackson broke up? Why didn't you leave it as it was and carry on with your life?"

"Because, I felt Jackson needed an honest reason behind our break up and not a lie. He deserved that. I came to you first in hopes that you would be able to help Jackson handle the situation. I know he is still very much in love with me."

"Hold up girl, I am not laying nothing like this on him! You got to do that yourself. And I don't want to be any part of it," Bill said while thinking about why he asked Jackson to come over in the first place. His mind was completely blank as far as Jackson was concerned. He knew his friend was going to be broken hearted again finding out the woman he was still in love with was gay. "Dang!" he moaned under his breath. Then he remembered why he invited Jackson over. He had Jerome Lockhart's address and he was going to ask Jackson if he wanted to pay him a visit to fight for the woman he loved. He knew Jackson really loved Carmella and if he could encourage him in a positive way he was going to do just that. But, now that Carmella had thrown a curveball, he wished the girl just went on and left Jackson alone.

Little did Carmella know, but she had just confirmed what Bill Tilmann thought of the black woman, always out to get her man and get him right where it hurts.

"She is no good!" he mumbled.

It brought back seriously bad memories of the hurt he felt with a woman name Doris Richardson. Oh yes, Doris was fine, intelligent, independent and everything he ever wanted in

Shérri A. Gambrill

a woman. He trusted this woman with his life and loved her totally with his heart and he knew she loved him and trusted him the same way. And now he had a half sister from Doris Richardson. She left him to share her love with his father who moved to California. William had an affair with Doris for four months before Bill ever found out and it wasn't from William Bill found out it was from Doris who couldn't take the deceit anymore.

This was part of his life he never shared with anyone, not even Jackson. He never tell his secret to anyone, he take it to his grave. This incident that was taking place in his home made his heart ache. It was like someone was sticking a knife deeper into a already deep wound.

"So when do you plan on telling Jackson this?" Bill asked in a dry tone.

"I'm going to call him tomorrow and talk to him. Maybe Jackson can go on with his life and forget about me," she stated while wiping a slowly driven tear from her eye. "I never wanted to hurt him Bill. Please believe that. If Jackson and I could be friends I would love that. But I don't think that is possible at this point."

"You're straight on that one," Bill stated while watching her.

She was so deceitful and wanted to come back into a man's life to destroy what little hope he had. Why didn't she just leave it alone and go on to doing whatever it was she was doing? Bill watched Carmella. He couldn't get a hand on it, but something was different about her.

Meanwhile Jackson finished his shower. "Man, after that shower I don't feel as drained. I think I'll pay my boy a visit after all," Jackson announced to himself as he stepped into a pair of jeans and slipped on a tee shirt. Then he clicked off the stereo and ran out the front door.

"Carmella I think you better go now, I have a lot of thinking to do," Bill stated wanting to just slap her face for hurting his friend a second time.

In But A Moment

"Please remember Bill you promised me you would not tell Jackson I was here. Is your promise still good?"

"Yes, my promise is still good. I don't want any part of this confusion anyway," Bill stated while gesturing Carmella to get up.

"Thank you Bill. You don't know what that means to me. I want to be able to tell Jackson in my own way and time. Thank you for respecting my request," she stated while holding on to the white leather sofa sitting in the middle of his living room. She slowly captured his entire room and noticed how decorative it was. For a man she liked his style and his concern for his friend.

She slowly walked over the thick white carpet and took a final look at his domain and thought what class he had. "Thanks for listening Bill, I really appreciated it."

Jackson sat in his car with his head on the steering wheel. He knew the car parked in Bill's driveway was Carmella's. As he was about to put the car in reverse he heard the front door of Bill's condo open and watched Carmella hug Bill in the doorway. Jackson was crushed his ex-woman was stroking his best friend and he was allowing it to happen. He wanted to cry while watching his beautiful Carmella walk to her car, with the biggest smile he had ever saw on her face.

"I can't believe this. Bill of all people. I would never think Bill would do me like that," Jackson mumbled to himself while watching Carmella pull out of Bill's driveway.

Bill walked back over to the sofa trying to absorb everything Carmella had just told him. He noticed a piece of material hanging from the arm of the sofa. "She left her scarf." Bill ran to the door to try and catch her. He swung the door open to call Carmella but it was too late. She had already pulled off. As he was about to shut the door he thought the dark color car parked across the street looked like Jackson's.

Bill took a closer look as he walked down the front steps of his condo. "That is Jackson. Man! I know he saw

Carmella leaving here." Bill ran down the front steps over to Jackson. He knocked on the window. Jackson slowly rolled the window down.

"Yeah, man what's up?" Jackson stated with the meanest look he could create on his face. He was so pissed he was afraid of what would happen between he and his best friend. He was trying very hard to keep his composure. "Look man I know you're pissed off right now, but it's not what you think. I can explain it all to you," Bill said.

"Man how can you possibly explain this to me? I saw her here and there is nothing you can say to me to make me understand her being here. And not only that I guess she was your company when I called, huh? You couldn't even tell me that. I think this whole thing is really messed up." Jackson snorted while trying to roll his window back up. Bill pushed on the window stopping him from rolling it up.

"Look man, you and I go way back I would never be that low and get it with your girl. Man you know I know how you feel about her and that you still love her. Just give a me a chance to explain," Bill begged with hurt in his eyes.

"All right spill it then," Jackson said.

"Get out the car and come inside. This may take a while."

Bill pulled on the front door proceeding to open the door for his friend. At that moment he forgot his promise to Carmella. He was going to tell Jackson everything. Jackson Water's was his best friend and he loved him like a brother.

7
I Love YOU So

"**O**kay Donna just ignore him. Act just like you don't see him," Nicole said while pulling at her sister's arm. Nicole thought to herself, how could he have the nerve to come here with some woman? "I can't believe this," she said. "Men, they are really something."

"What's wrong with you two? Come on!" Michelle screamed over the loud music blasting in the background.

"Hold up, David is here with a woman and Donna is very upset," Nicole told Michelle and Stacie.

"See I told y'all they ain't nothing but dogs! All of them. He couldn't even wait until he forgot about Donna to go bringing some other woman all up in here. He don't care nothing about your feelings or he wouldn't be up here with some woman. I told you girl, you should forget about him. He ain't even worth the heartache and pain."

"First, of all y'all don't even know what's up with David. Y'all don't know who that is he's sitting with. Don't assume that's his new lady," Stacie said.

"Girl, that's bull! He ain't brought no woman to no club wanting to just chit chat! He could have taken her home for that. Especially with all this blasting music going on."

"If I were you Donna I'd go over there and say hello," Stacie suggested.

"Girl, don't make no fool out of yourself by going over there. I'd let him know two can play that game! I'd be all up in some brother's face giving him a taste of his own medicine," Michelle stated while signaling the waitress over to order a gin and tonic.

"You do what you feel is comfortable for you Donna. No matter what anyone says, if you feel uncomfortable being here we can go," Stacie told her friend. No matter what the

45

situation was Stacie knew Donna was hurt and just wanted to cry.

Michelle interrupted her thoughts. "Girl, what you talking about we are not staying, not after I just gave my ten dollars up. The hell with that!"

"Well Michelle you can stay if you like. I can get a jitney and take Donna home." Nicole looked at her sister and wanted to go right over to David and throw her drink right in his face for being so disrespectful.

"You know what, I think I will go home," Donna stated through tear stained eyes. But you guys stay I can get a jitney by myself."

"No," Nicole said. "I'll go with you."

"No, I mean it. You all stay. I like to be myself anyway. Don't worry. I am not that naive to do something crazy. You know me better than that. You guys go a head and enjoy the night." Donna's sister and friends hugged her and told her they would see her when they got home. Michelle had already seized her eyes on a brother sitting at the bar.

"Please y'all don't say anything to David, don't let him know I was here or that I saw him okay?"

"Okay, sweetie I'll wait outside with you until your jitney comes," Nicole told her sister. Stacie had called a jitney for Donna and went searching for Michelle. Nicole walked her sister outside. Donna turned to face her sister as the tears sprang from her eyes.

"Oh Nicole why? Why? I know we were broken up and I shouldn't even care or be concerned about who David decides to date, but it hurts so bad to see him with someone else." She wiped her eyes as deep groans of pain escaped her. Then she leaned on the pole outside of the club as her whole body shook uncontrollably. She worried how she would survive without the one man she truly loved with all her heart.

In But A Moment

"Come here sweetie," Nicole said holding her sister in her arms. "It will be all right." Nicole continued embracing her sister while feeling bad because she knew that Donna really loved David. Nicole wiped Donna's tears away but could feel her own feelings begin to emerge. She felt the same lump in her throat as her sister did. She wanted so much for Donna to feel better because she hated seeing her in that condition. Donna and David were so good together and she knew her sister missed him terribly. She wanted more than anything to smooth things out for her. She only wished she had had the opportunity to experience something so wonderful. Why did it have to hurt so much? How could she help her? All she really wanted was David so what could she say to make her feel better? She rubbed her back as Donna looked up at her with red eyes.

"Oh Nicole I love that man so much. I miss him. I miss his touch, his laughter, his smile, his hugs, our friendship…. I miss him so much Nicole," Donna said while resting her head back on her sister's shoulder. "I love him. I love him so much," she cried causing a chain reaction of tears to fall.

Suddenly, the sound of a car horn made Donna lift her head to see a bright red four-door sedan waiting across the street.

"Are you sure you don't want me to come with you Donna?" Nicole asked her glassy eyed sister.

Donna sniffed and wiped her eyes with the tissue Nicole handed her "Yes, I am sure. You go ahead in and have fun. I'll be okay. Really I will," Donna assured her sister. Then she turned and walked toward the red car waiting for her and climbed in. She waved good-bye to her with a half way pretend smile and wondered what life had in store for her without the man she loved being part of it.

"Where to lady?" the jitney driver asked.

"221 Coal Street," she said resting her head against the hard leather seat. She cried all the way home while the driver watched her in the rearview mirror.

As he peered at her, visions of her broken heart filled the car. Then he thought about how pretty she was and how much she reminded him of his own daughter. Even though the drive was quiet and sort of tense, his assumptions of her problems created quite an array of unspoken conversation. And before they knew it, the jitney driver was pulling up to the apartment complex. Without a second thought, he got out the car to help her out.

Donna paid the fare, thanked the driver and walked up the steps to her apartment. She opened the small leather bag she was carrying and searched for the keys to her apartment. She unlocked the door and kicked off her shoes. She thought to herself, now you have to control yourself it's not worth getting this upset. After all you and David are not together anymore therefore he is free to see whomever he likes. Donna walked into her black and gold bathroom and removed her coat and dress. She began to wash her makeup off and took a good look at herself. She could feel the swell of tears form at her eyes and finally drop on the gold porcelain sink. She slipped on her robe, walked into the kitchen and poured herself a glass of white wine to help her relax.

"David I miss you so much," she whispered to herself as she embraced her body with her arms. She couldn't believe David would involve himself with someone so quickly. She wondered what it was that they had.

She went out onto the terrace and watched the stars dance brightly against the blacken sky. She smiled to herself as she remembered the times she and David shared on that very terrace watching the black sky and diamond shaped stars. Finally she decided to go to bed, a good night sleep was what she really wanted and after drinking the wine.

8
<u>In a twinkling of an eye</u>

" **C**an you believe David, Girl?" Nicole told Stacie as she watched David with wicked eyes. David sat there listening to the woman go on and on about how she had seen him several times at the club and didn't have the nerve to come up to him until now.

While she talked on and on David was thinking of Donna. He had missed her and he had made a mental note to stop the confusion as far as he and she were concern. He was going to call her as soon as he could get away from motor mouth. He realized that she was a good woman.

He played with the straw in his glass, stirring his drink while little bubbles circulated around the edges. He was lucky to have found Donna and though they had their arguments now and then it was never anything worth breaking up over. He could understand how Donna could be upset with him. Who was he to tell her who she could continue being friends with? Her independence was what attracted him to her in the first place.

David watched the girl who was seated across from him. His stare was so intense that he felt as if he could see straight through her. He didn't want to hurt her feelings and though she was very attractive he just wasn't interested in her. She seemed to be very intelligent from her conversation. She sat there trying to seduce him with her eyes.

"You know we haven't even introduced ourselves and I'm just sitting here burning up a storm with you."

"Hi. I'm Donna," she said while extending a manicured hand.

David drifted forward to the present as he focused on the pretty girl sitting across from him. "Oh," he said, "I'm David." He pondered how much of a coincidence it was that her name happened to be Donna. Maybe fate was trying to tell him something.

"Well David, I am pleased to meet you," she said smiling at him with prefect teeth. The sounds of reggae music swaddled the room and Donna swayed back and forth in her chair to the beat. "Hey you wanted dance?"

"Not really maybe later. I'm just not in the mood right now."

"Awe come on! You look as though you need a little cheering up. If you dance with me it will help you loosen up some. You're suppose to be having fun, not looking as though you lost your best friend." The woman reached across the table and look at David with her light green eyes. Softly she touched his arm. "Please?" she pleaded while positioning her lips in such a way to cause a pout.

"Okay, yes I'll dance with you," he said while pushing his chair back from the table.

Donna watched him as he stood up and she studied how handsome, and masculine looked. Her taste in appearance always led her to well-dressed men. And he was definitely very well dressed. She immediately examined his shoes, basing her final decision on their condition. Then and only then would she be able to assume he was a bona fide well dresser. She stood up while repositioning her dress in its proper position and walked over to his side of the table checking him out thoroughly. She let her eyes travel down his body slowly until she got to his shoes with fingers crossed behind her back.

"Yes," she shouted with silent joy while continuing to move to the beat of the music. Slowly she grabbed David's hand.

Nicole sat at the bar watching David like a hawk. And she could feel her stomach churning. To her, the whole scene was piteous. She was to the point where she wanted to throw up.

In But A Moment

"Hey lady would you like to dance?" asked a tall and sort of goofy looking man.

Nicole looked at him as if he didn't deserve to be on the same earth as she. But then after evaporating her attitude towards the man, she changed her mind. "Yes." She wanted David to see her on the dance floor and she was going to make it her business for him to do just that.

They squeezed passed the crowd and moved their way to the dance floor, which was so crowed they could barely move themselves. The goofy brother moved closer to Nicole to ask her name. "Beverly, my friends call me Bev," she lied.

"My name is Robert my friends call me Rob. And I do want you to be my friend," he said while trying to come across as sexy. But instead he demonstrated how obnoxious he could be.

Nicole looked at him with all his fancy jewelry and whispered various questions under her breath. "Why God? Why me all the time?" she asked smiling at the man and shaking her head.

Robert smiled thinking the gesture she gave was an invitation for him to come closer and put his hands around her waist.

"Excuse me!" she said. But he just smiled as though he never heard her.

"What's a fine lady like yourself doing in this joint alone?"

"Who said I was alone?" she asked while rolling her eyes with disgust and pushing his hands away from her waist.

"Okay, thanks for the dance," she told him as she proceeded to move off the dance floor.

"Anytime. I hope to get another."

"Not in this life time," she whispered. Then she fought her way back through the crowd and saw Michelle and Stacie signaling her to their newfound table. With relief in her step, she smiled and proceeded over.

"Dang! Who was the fly brother you were dancing with?" Michelle asked laughing.

"Girl, please! I just wanted to get on that dance floor to see David. He didn't see me though. I guess I couldn't get his attention. It was too crowded."

"Hello ladies, how's everyone this evening? Are you enjoying yourselves?"

All three ladies turned to find David standing before them. Silence lasted but a moment.

"How are we doing? How the hell you doing? I guess just fine," Michelle said while twisting her body to face David. "We see you couldn't wait to be all up in some other woman's face."

"Excuse me? What are you talking about Michelle?"

"All come on David. Stop the innocent act. We saw you all up in that woman's face. She has her 'I'm looking for a man' game face on."

"What are you talking about? I was not in that woman's face. She was all up in my face."

"Yeah right, how does the saying go? A bird of a feather flocks together. In this case all dogs are alike except for the bark. And to me, you look like you were barking your mouth off." Michelle put her hand up to David's face to prevent any form of language from escaping his lips. "I ain't hearing it," she announced.

David removed himself from the back of Michelle's hand and proceeded to speak. "Don't put me in a category of your other so called men," David said as frustration began to set in.

"Is that your new lady?" Stacie asked innocently.

"No that isn't! I don't even know that girl. Anyway I just wanted to come over to speak. I didn't know I was going to be interrogated for holding a completely innocent conversation with someone I don't even know."

"I'm sure you know her now." Michelle stated with fury in her voice.

He proceeded to walk away because he knew what was about to happen. They were ready to chew him completely up and he just wasn't in the mood to hear it.

Remotely, Stacie urged him to stick around a little longer. "Aren't you even concerned about Donna? I mean, like where she is?"

David turned abruptly to face Stacie. "Finally, someone who could be a little civil," he said with still lips. "Yes as a matter of fact I was going to asked but everyone was so busy trying to tell me who my new woman was. What was the need? So where is she?" he asked, hoping they were going to tell him she was in the ladies room or something.

Nicole kicked Stacie under the table to let her know she knew what she was about to do. Stacie ignored her kick and spoke anyway. "She was with us, but she left."

"Why?" he asked.

"Because. Why would she want to sit up in here with your tired behind all up in some other woman's face?" Michelle asked with a strong voice. "Basically David, she was very upset when she saw you. She assumed that you were with that woman so she went home in tears."

"Man! I really didn't want Donna to see me with anyone. Had I known…."

"Had you known Donna was going to be here you would have taken your woman elsewhere to entertain her," Michelle conveniently acknowledged.

David's temper was about to explode right in Michelle's face. But before he would allow that to happen he ignored her and faced Stacie once again.

"I really need to see my baby", he stated as a hopeful request.

"All you need to do is take your tired butt on, and leave Donna alone," Michelle stated.

At that moment, both Stacie and Nicole told Michelle to shut up. Then they assured David that he needed to do what he needed to do.

"You still love her don't you David?" Stacie asked. Both Nicole and Stacie knew the answer to the question.

"Yes, I never stopped. Nicole, do me a favor. Give me the key to the apartment so I can get in and try to explain to Donna about this evening. I know she won't let me in if I just go knocking on the door."

"If she got any sense, she won't let you in at all," Michelle stated solidly.

Nicole, with a sense of compassion, told him that he knew where the spare was. She didn't want to give him her key for fear of interrupting them once David got in the apartment. She couldn't imagine having to ring the doorbell. "Good luck," she stated.

"Thanks babe, I owe you big time."

"And you know I," Nicole screamed after him.

Michelle sat looking at her two friends. "Why y'all tell me to shut up? Donna doesn't need his tired butt." She drew her attention back to enjoying the club atmosphere. "Come on y'all, are we playing this game or what? Or am I on my own?"

Since Stacie and Nicole were on one accord, both women looked at Michelle and shook their heads. Since they shared the confidence that he really loved her and they prayed that David and Donna would get back together, they loved the idea that he was going to her. After all, she really needed him.

"Girl the brothers are up in here tonight," Michelle stated interrupting both Stacie and Nicole's thoughts. Michelle danced to the rhythm while sitting in her seat as a barmaid approached them and asked if they needed anything.

"Yes, I'll take another gin and tonic," Michelle said without a second thought.

"Just white wine for me," Nicole said

"And tonic and lemon for me," Stacie said.

"Okay I'll be back in a jiffy."

That night the club was very crowded. In fact it was more crowded than usual. There was a thick ambiance among the people as everyone went about their natural way. The woman David had been with earlier was now standing next to a very muscular, dark man and he was positioned in her face as though he were telling her off. She was trying to ignore him as best she could without being too obvious.

Stacie watched the scene from her seat while Nicole had gone to the ladies room. Michelle of course was on the dance floor dancing and doing what she intended, having a good time. Stacie began to play with the straw in her glass, which was now leaning on the opposite side. From the moment it took for Stacie to look up from her glass she heard it. The blaring sound of screams, she jumped to her feet and witnessed the man standing with the woman David had just left, aiming a gun to the dance floor. And in that brief period of time, he began to fire the weapon randomly. Stacie's instinct was to lay on the floor or hide under the table as people ran in all directions. With a sense of urgency, security rushed in and tackled the man to the floor. Stacie could hear him screaming.

"Don't play me as a fool! If I can't have you none of these suckers will!"

"Oh my God", Stacie whispered under her breath. She was shaking all over when suddenly she spotted Nicole coming out of the ladies room. She screamed her name at the top of her lungs. "Nicole, hurry!"

Nicole, unaware of the situation, ran to join her under the table. "Oh my god, what happened?"

"I'm not sure," she said while grasping for breath. She could feel her heart pounding so hard she thought it would explode. I saw this guy talking to that girl that was with David. Then all of a sudden he just started shooting onto the dance floor. She grabbed her friend's hand as both women continued to stay under the table.

"Did the girl know him?" Nicole asked beginning to feel an awful fear run through her body.

"I guess. I don't know. Maybe. Oh God, I want to go home. I'm scared," she told her friend while continuing to hold her hand. She paused as she allowed her lips to quiver. "It appeared as though she knew him. They looked as though they were in some type of disagreement. Oh Nicole! Oh my god," she cried as a revelation came to her. She was still holding onto her hand as she thought about the question that she wanted to ask.

"Where's Michelle? Michelle, where is Michelle?" Nicole asked again as tears sprang from her eyes.

"Oh no, Stacie please. Please. Oh God! Stacie please don't tell me Michelle is on that dance floor." She cried and reached up to grip the tabletop that they were under. As she scanned around, she saw police officers everywhere. Then she was startled when she saw the horrific sight of several people lying on the floor. Suddenly, the sounds of voices sent a chill down her spine.

"Over here, over here get an ambulance quick or else we are going to loose this one. She's been shot in the head."

As Nicole stood up and saw the pandemonium in the club, she stepped closer to the scene. Then through the dim lights she saw the deep red reflection of her friend's memories. Blood oozed from Michelle's head. Nicole opened her eyes wide and froze with fear. With a delayed reaction, she screamed and covered her mouth with her hand. "No! No! Oh God, Michelle. Oh my god, Michelle!" Without hesitation, she ran to her friend who now lay limp on the floor with a pool of blood around her. To Nicole, Michelle looked to be dead. "Oh God please don't let her be dead. God please don't let…." She whimpered softly as she cried and knew deep in her heart she had already lost her friend. Bravely crawling over to Michelle, she decided to hug her and lay her head in her chest. "Oh Michelle I love you." As the bright lights flashed on, all she could do was cry softly as the police and the few other people who were left in the club looked on.

Finally the paramedics arrived and ran to Michelle and the four other bodies that lay on the floor.

"Please sir is she going to live? Please, sir, don't let her die. Please. I love her. She's my friend. Please don't die Michelle," she pleaded. "Please, I need you. Don't die. Hold on please." Nicole screamed and began hitting the floor as she watched the man in the white suit work on her friend.

"I am sorry Miss. She's gone."

Nicole looked on the floor, but she couldn't manage to focus on what was real.

"What is this? What just happened? Things needed to slow down, everything is moving too fast." She began to realize that she was permitting a strange man to inform her of the awful reality. "This isn't true. Not Michelle, God no, not Michelle. No, she's not dead," she murmured while shaking her head vigorously. Then Nicole cried to him as she pulled on his arm. "No, she can't be. Please do something."

The man watched her and his heart sank for her. He knew it was a senseless murder of an innocent young girl just out having a good time with her friends and now she was dead. He could see that the young woman holding on to his arm really loved her friend. She was a mess and he knew it was going to be a rough road ahead trying to accept her friend's death. It was all so senseless. Stacie was watching closely from the table as she felt a hand touch her.

"Miss are you okay?" asked a mild voice.

Stacie looked up at the man standing before her. "Please can you tell me if that girl laying on the floor is going to be okay?" She already knew in her heart that Michelle was dead, but she just needed to hear it from somebody else. She knew the minute she saw Nicole collapsed in the paramedic's arms. The young man helped her up and walked her over to where Nicole was as Stacie stood back and watched.

Realizing what was confirmed now she fell to the floor and cried for the loss of both her friends as she asked herself why. Why did everyone that she loved have to die? She

watched Nicole holding Michelle's limp body. She thought
life was just but a minute and how precious it really was.

"I love you Michelle."

She whispered as she walked over to Nicole. Nicole
looked up and embraced Stacie, crying in her arms for what
seemed like hours. Stacie knew at that point how much their
lives were going to change and how much she would have to
be there for Nicole. She also knew that she would have to be
extra strong to carry the weight of her sorrows. But at that
moment being strong was something she couldn't do. So she
hugged Nicole and wept softly in her bosom.

9
<u>My Brother</u>

J ackson followed his friend to the front door and proceeded to sit on the white cushioned sofa. "All right man what's the deal?" Jackson asked while watching Bill grab two beers from the fridge.

"Man, I don't know how to break this to you."

"Just do it man. Just do it," Jackson said beginning to get even angrier.

Bill watched his friend from the corner of his eyes and tried to figure the best way to say what he knew would break his heart. "Man, I don't know how to break this to you, but Carmella came here for one reason and one reason only."

"Yeah I know," Jackson mumbled under his breath.

"Jackson, she came to tell me that she was gay. She had lied to you and me all this time. She isn't seeing Jerome. Jerome is her cousin. She's living with Denise and apparently she and Denise have been shacking up. They are both gay. It caught me by surprise too. Man I couldn't believe it."

Jackson laughed out loud as he placed his hands on his head. "Man you have got to be out of your mind. Who in the hell do you think you are talking to? Man, Carmella ain't nowhere near gay. Come on," he stated while walking over to his friend.

Bill could see the pain in his face but in addition to that he noticed a different demeanor about Jackson. It was one he had never seen before. It looked as though he despised him for a split second and Bill couldn't determine if it was because of the news he had just told him or if Jackson truly did not believe him. He just couldn't put his finger on it but he knew that it bothered him a great deal. Just as he was about to go into specific details his doorbell rang. Jackson looked at his friend.

"Who is that? Another one of your so called women?"

"I don't know," Bill stated looking startled. He slowly walked over to the door and opened it to see Carmella back again. "What is it Carmella?"

"Oh I am sorry to disturb you again Bill but I think I left my scarf here. Did you see it?"

Bill told her to stay there and he would bring it to her. But as Bill walked away Darletta followed him and was stunned to see Jackson.

"Jackson, what are you doing here?" she questioned looking totally distraught.

Jackson watched her closely as he felt the burning desire to just grab her and tell her how much he truly missed and loved her. Bill approached the room scolding Carmella for ignoring his request for her to wait outside. Meanwhile, Darletta continued ignoring him and watched Jackson.

"Damn. How am I going to get out of this one?" echoed the question in her mouth. "For some reason I believe big mouth Bill has run his mouth."

Bill confirmed her suspension. "Carmella, Jackson knows everything. So please just go."

She looked at Bill and rolled her eyes. "How could you hurt Jackson like that, Bill?"

How could I hurt Jackson?" he asked with a humorous tone. "Girl please you have done enough hurt for one night. Please just leave."

Okay, I'll leave."

Darletta walked over to Jackson and touched his heart with her eyes. "I am sorry he hurt you Jackson, but I came to ask Bill if he could please find a way to tell you that I still loved you and wanted you back. He confessed to me that he loved me and always did. He also told me that he was going to tell you as soon as I left. I don't love him Jackson I still love you please give me a chance to really prove myself. Please," Darletta stated hugging Jackson with all her might. Through all of the drama, her goal was to produce real tears.

In But A Moment

"Why you witch!" Bill had never in his whole entire life retorted to calling a woman out of her name. And it hurt him to have to do it at that moment. But because everything was a lie, he grew bitter and angry. "I can't believe this. Jackson I know darn well you are not going to believe this bull! Man come on," Bill stated pleading with his friend.

Jackson looked at Bill. "Man I always knew you cared a little to much for Carmella but to want her for yourself and then go behind my back to try and get her is low. That's really messed up." Jackson, never felt the type of pain he was feeling right at that moment. He didn't want to believe Carmella. He also wanted to trust his friend for he had never given him a reason not to. But Carmella had never lied to him either. The difference was he loved his friend, but he was in love with the woman who stood beside him and that love was rooted deep in his being.

Jackson held Darletta as she smiled in his chest and slowly caressed his back. "Come on Carmella let me take you home and you can tell me all the details."

Bill watched his friend and couldn't believe what he just saw. Here was someone whom he loved like a brother and he was turning his back on him not even listening to what he was saying. He was that much in love with a woman that he would let it damage their friendship. Then thoughts of slapping Carmella's face entered his mind. It wasn't so much for lying but for dissolving the friendship he shared with Jackson. Bill watched, as his friend left with the woman who he could not believe had just lied right to his face. He couldn't believe how much Carmella had changed. He never thought she had it in her to be so deceitful and mean. His opinion of her was different now and worse, he knew Jackson was so in love with the woman that he couldn't even see the change in her. Bill would never forgive her for what she had done to his friendship with Jackson. Feeling frustrated and confused, he walked to his bedroom and turned on his jazz

CD. He closed his eyes and thought what he had to do next to win his friend back.

David pulled up in front of the red brick building that Nicole and Donna shared. He parked his car right in front and looked up at the window that faced the street. He noticed there were no lights on. He wondered now if maybe it was a mistake to have come. Maybe Donna was so hurt and angry she didn't want to see him.

Well, that was a chance he was just going to have to take. He loved Donna and this time he was going to prove just that to her. She was his life and he always felt so good when he was with her. It was time for him to let her know exactly how he felt and show her just how much he really loved her.

He turned the engine off, stepped out of the car and climbed the steps to the condo. He wasn't sure what Donna's reaction was going to be towards him, but he'd take his chances. He rang the doorbell five times, but Donna never answered. Then he remembered what Nicole said about the spare key. He hoped that it was still there. He kneeled down to look under the mat and sure enough there it was. David kissed the key and smiled.

He didn't see Donna anywhere so he checked the bedroom. There she was lying across the bed holding her pillow and looking beautiful. She was still wearing the gold and black robe that he had brought her for Christmas last year. David stood in the doorway of her bedroom and watched her as she slept.

He slowly removed his shoes and clothes and walked over to her bed, pulled the covers back and slid in next to her. He snuggled up close to her from behind and wrapped his arms around her. Donna did not move one inch at first, until David began to kiss her face and she could hear him telling her how much he loved her.

"David, what are you doing here?"

"I love you Donna and I was such a fool. I don't want to loose you," he told her as he held her in his arms.

In But A Moment

"Are you still mad at me baby?"

"Oh baby! No I'm not mad. I missed you, but I thought you didn't want me anymore. I saw you with that woman at the club David."

"Sweetheart, I just went there to get a drink to try and relax because I was so down about you and I having that stupid argument. I love baby. I really do and whatever it takes to prove that I will."

Gently he began to bite her lips. Then he separated her lips with his tongue and caressed her tongue with his and explored the avenues of her mouth with his. He knew he really truly loved this woman, she was everything to him. He was never going to be childish when it came to Donna Ausha Grant.

"I've missed you baby", he said as he continued to stroke her body.

10
<u>Let the Games Begin</u>

J ackson reached for Carmella's hand as he escorted her
down the steps of Bill's condo. "Oh Jackson, I almost
forgot, you can't drive me home I have my car," she
stated while watching Jackson's face.

"Right," he said. "I almost forgot myself. I was so
caught up in the conversation Bill was having with me. "I'll
tell you what, you follow me back to my place. I'd like to
really hear your side of the story Carmella. I mean, after all
you have to admit that was some heavy stuff that Bill just laid
on me. I just can't believe he would try something like this.
He knew how I felt about you. I've never known him to do
something like this." He watched her for any impression or
comment she might have. She never responded. She just
continued walking towards her car. He reached for her hand.

"Baby, you deserve to express your side of the story.
And I want to hear what you have to say," he said touching
her gently on her back.

"I know," she answered, while flashing back to the
conversation that just took place 20 minutes ago in Bill's
condo. Darletta needed some time to think out her next plan
and quickly. "Jackson, I'll tell you what, I'll stop by your
place after I run by my apartment okay? I have to take care of
a few things."

"All right fine. I'll see you in about 30 minutes or so,"
he said while looking at his watch.

"Yes," she replied. "I'll see you then." She reached
up and kissed Jackson on his cheek.

Darletta pulled into the parking lot of her sister's
apartment complex. She needed some time. Things were
surely moving a tad bit to quickly for her. How stupid she
was to go back to Bill's place. Had she not, she would not
have run into Jackson Waters. Now she was in a position of

coming up with another plan to persuade Mr. Water's that she was her perfect sister Carmella Springer. She laid her head back for a moment or two to collect her thoughts for her next actions. "What do I say to Mr. Waters? Or what do I do to convince this man that I am who I say I am?"

She pushed herself out of the small car and proceeded to her sister's apartment. Once inside the building she walked over to the elevator and pushed the button. "This elevator is taking forever to get down here," she snapped. The elevator doors bounced opened. "Finally," she whispered, as she pushed past a tall stout woman looking at her with an irritable expression on her face. "The word is excuse me!" she announced to Darletta while positioning herself towards her.

"Well, you're excused!" Darletta snarled back at her.

"Ignorant fool," the woman stated more to herself than to Darletta.

Darletta heard the last comment right before the elevator doors were about to shut. She placed her hand in such a way to alleviate the closure and yelled at the woman. "It takes one to know one!" she screamed while allowing the elevator doors to close. Once arriving on her designated floor, she fumbled for her set of keys and then turned the door handle. She walked into the colorful apartment and kicked her shoes off to relax. Then she walked to the kitchen and poured herself a tall glass of white wine. "Maybe I won't go over to Jackson's tonight," she sighed. "I need this time to think of what I should do next, but then again, I should go over there since the brother is so heartbroken. This would be a grand opportunity to suck him right into the plan." She whispered to herself while laughing and gulping down the white wine.

After three additional glasses of wine she decided to go over there and just lay it on him in more ways than one. The wine made her a little light headed, but she was relaxed and ready to do what was necessary. She walked to the bathroom and splashed water on her face and brushed her teeth. Then she brushed her jet-black hair and pulled it up high on her head. After deciding that she was fine, she grabbed her purse from the couch and headed for the door. Suddenly, the ringing of the phone caused her to stop before opening the door.

"Dang! That's probably Jackson calling to see what's taking me so long. He'll see me when I get there," she said waving her hand at the phone. Darletta was half way down the hall, when the answering machine clicked on and allowed Carmella's voice to illuminated the room.

"Hi Darletta it's me, just seeing how things were going. I hope your staying out of trouble," she said in a laughing tone. "I miss you." She was just about to hang up when she remembered something. "Oh yeah, I hope you were able to get in touch with Jackson, to let him know where I am and that I love him. Also I hope you were able to let him know why I couldn't tell him I was leaving. I know it has been two weeks and all, but this is the first chance I've had to call. I really do miss him. Please Darletta, don't forget to tell him I'm sorry about the misunderstanding about Jerome. Thanks Sweetie. I'll talk to you soon. Chow."

Carmella sat back on her bed in the Hotel room. She really missed everyone, especially Jackson. She was practically demanded to work the flight going to China. How grateful, she was that her twin sister was able to leave Los Angeles at such a short notice to watch her apartment. Carmella's escapade would last at least a month, and Darletta was free for travel for a month, before her next shoot in the Caribbean. Carmella felt sorry for her sister because she really didn't have friends and the time that she had would be a prime opportunity for her to meet some. She thought maybe after Darletta explained everything to Jackson, he might be willing to show her around and introduce her to some people.

Though she really missed Jackson and couldn't wait to straighten everything out, she still needed her space to think. So much had happened. She felt bad about the break up, but it was the only way for her to keep things into perspective. She couldn't afford all the questions Jackson would surely have for her once he found out. She made a promise to her sister and she was going to keep it. She really hated Jerome Lockhart, but it was the only name she could say to Jackson since he was the only other man she had had a relationship with. And besides Jackson knew how close she and Jerome were at one time.

Carmella knew her sister was a sweet person deep down inside. But so much had happened to her to change her. How could she possibly think she could ever forgive her? Darletta and Carmella had been so much alike at one time and they spent every given moment together. Now all that had changed, and she now wondered if it would ever happen again. She also knew how angry her sister was with her. She felt in her heart that Darletta would do whatever to make her pay for the pain she had caused her.

And here Carmella was tied into a promise she knew she could never break. No matter how much Darletta tried to hurt her, she would always be her sister and she would always love her. For as long as she lived, the secret she and her sister shared would never be disclosed no matter what the circumstances were. She loved her sister, but she knew deep down Darletta had never forgiven her. She owed it to her sister to be as supportive as possible. Whatever Darletta asked of Carmella she was going to do. For she felt she owed her that much considering the pain she had gone through.

11
<u>Faith</u>

Stacie and Nicole rode in the back of the ambulance as the loud siren screamed through the streets. Neither woman was sure what to think when they heard the paramedic announce that he had a heartbeat. All they could think of was the slim reality their friend may be alive. For Nicole, alive was all she needed to hear.

Stacie on the other hand was not sure if Michelle's chance of life was worth the pain they would all suffer for not having her completely back. She knew in the depths of her soul that her friend was going to change.

Stacie watched Nicole as she whimpered softly in her bosom. "Please Michelle hang in there. We need you."

Stacie watched her friend closely for Nicole was so despondent. How would she react to Michelle living as a vegetable? How else would she survive? Stacie was so confused she felt she should be grateful that God has spared her friend regardless of what state was in. She was their friend and they would continue to love her no matter how the horrible incident turned out.

Then wondered why would God allow Michelle to suffer if it was in his plan to have her live as a vegetable? She didn't understand. "Maybe God is trying to tell us something through Michelle. I don't know," she whispered to herself. She was drained, distressed, angry and regretful for going out at all. If only she could take it all back and start over.

She cried deep sobs as she watched her friend fighting for her life and the friend who sat beside her. Then she remembered a passage her mother had said so many times. And for some reason it became so clear to her. "If you have faith the size of a mustard seed you can move mountains." Stacie produced a small smile across her face. She knew she had that faith her mother had spoken of and she had the ability to use it. Just thinking of the passage made her long for her mother.

In But A Moment

For some reason her desire to reach for her mother was so evident. She was real through the touch of her emotions and now she needed to touch her mother. And when she did she heard her saying the passage she repeated to herself. She knew there was going to be hope because of the faith her mother spoke so divinely of. She began to say a silent prayer asking God to please spear her friend and help her to deal with any situation dealing with Michelle.

When she completed her pray she felt a soft stroke against her back moving in a circular motion, and for a minute she was content to believe it was one of the paramedics just comforting her as her eyes were closed. She opened her eyes and realized both paramedics were generating their energies towards Michelle and were far away from her. For that moment she knew in her heart what the stroke was, it was her mother right there beside her, letting her know she would never leave her. She was her baby and she would always watch over her.

Stacie felt a warm gentle peacefulness build up inside her and as quickly as she felt it she felt her emotions come to the surface. And for the first time in a long time she broke down. The whole episode made her heart ache with excruciating pain.

Her mother's love was surely generating inside her and she longed to keep it there forever. She looked at her two friends and wanted to pass the love she was feeling to them. For that moment she knew what it was to really truly love, for she knew it was right there in back of that ambulance. She laid her head back, closed her eyes and thought how in a moment so much had changed forever.

The ambulance came to a rushing stop and both Nicole and Stacie sat up as the back door swung open. The paramedics swished out the back of the ambulance while hanging onto Michelle's stretcher. Both women heard the young man who told them their friend was dead.

"Coming through, gun shot victim!"

Shérri A. Gambrill

Doctors and nurses came from everywhere to assist in any way they could. A dark haired, thin woman in a white uniform approached both women and helped them to the waiting area of the hospital.

Hours had passed before anyone came to acknowledge Nicole and Stacie. From what Stacie could gather, they were taking Michelle straight to the operating room to try and remove the bullet. Nicole had laid her head in her friend's lap and breathed softly to the rhythm of her broken heart. She had to call Donna to let her know what had happened. Although it was now 5:00 AM, she knew Donna had to know what had happened. Even though she had no news to tell her of Michelle's condition, she felt she still needed to know. Then she remembered while walking towards the phone that David was trying to reconcile with Donna. And knowing David he probably succeeded in doing just that.

"Let her savor the moment," she spoke aloud. "Let her enjoy the joyful escapade."

A sincere smile caressed her face. She knew in her heart and soul Michelle was going to make it and be complete. So she figured she would tell Donna when she got the necessary information about Michelle's condition.

She began to walk slowly back to where Nicole now laid in the waiting area sound asleep. "Sleep well my friend it's going to be okay."

12
Let the Birds Sing

T he bright sun illuminated the room where Donna and
David were. Donna still enjoyed the tingling feeling she
felt as she reminisced about their night of love.
Although she felt so wonderfully secure as she watched her
man lay beside her, she felt as though something was not quite
right. She just couldn't put her finger on it.

David snored lightly as Donna absorbed the brightness
of the sun and the birds singing so sweetly. She watched
David breath while tracing his face with her fingertips. She
wanted the moment to last forever. David lying beside her,
peaceful in his sleep, and her observing every inch of his
body.

Life was so prefect and nothing was going to spoil the
already beautiful day. While all seemed so prefect to her there
still was something that tugged at her heart in an
unconventional manner. She decided to brush it off and
continue enjoying her treasures. David never moved as she
reached over and kissed him gently on his check.

She smiled as she continued to replay their love
making over in her mind. He was a loving man and she was
glad he came back to her apologizing and making things right
again.

She turned the shower on, removed her silk robe and
stepped into the pulsating water. She knew David would sleep
at least another hour. Therefore she had time to shower and
start breakfast.

He rolled over to reach for Donna and instead felt the
smoothness of the satin sheets. Once he had his composure he
realized she was taking a shower and smiled. He removed
himself from the satin sheets and decided he would join his
girl in a shower. He slipped on a robe Donna kept at the
condo for him when he spent the night and walked towards the

bathroom. Once he invited himself into the bathroom he pulled back the shower curtain.

"David, what are you doing in here I thought you were asleep? Did I wake you?"

"Nah, well I guess maybe you did. That scent I smelled was so refreshing and pretty I had to see what you were doing. Mind if I join you?"

"Come on in baby, but no funny stuff. We might wake Nicole."

"Okay," he said smiling. "Come here girl and let me wash your body."

"David you are so crazy," she teased as she pushed him away. "Come on baby lets not start something we can't finish," she told him while continuing to push him away.

"Who says we can't finish?" he said with a sly smile.

"I do, we're going to wake Nicole. I know she must be tired. She had to have gotten in really late or should I say very early? She must have had a great time. I'm glad. Maybe this time she met someone worthwhile. Although I can't imagine that happening considering the club thing is so weak," she said while grabbing a towel. "I wish she could find someone like you honey. I'm so blessed to have you all to myself."

"Don't worry baby, Nicole will find someone. She just needs to stop looking so hard. It will happen when she least expects it. One day someone is going to appreciate what it is she has to offer. You'll see. Trust me I know about these things," he told her while grabbing her back under the running water and kissing her.

"I know baby, you're right. What can I say?"

"Come here. You don't have to say a word," he told her while pulling her wet body close to him. "What is that scent?"

"Oh you like huh?"

"Yes!"

"I love you," she said as she kissed him.

In But A Moment

"Are you happy baby?"
"Very! The birds woke me singing."

13
A Second Chance

Jackson jumped when he heard the knock on the door. He thought Carmella had changed her mind about coming over. After all, it was late. Although it didn't matter what time it was when she got there he was going to let her in. He had her back in his life and nothing was going to get in the way of their reunion. He had just begun to doze off when he heard the knock on the door.

"Yeah?" he said waiting for a response.

"Hi baby, it's me. Open up." Jackson opened the door and invited Carmella in.

"Hey," he said. "I thought maybe you changed your mind."

"Oh no baby I just wanted to get a little refreshed. I told you I had to take care of something right?"

"Oh yeah, so what was it you had to take care of?" he asked.

He sure is a nosey somebody, she thought to herself. She didn't think it was any of his business but instead of saying it she just smiled and told him it wasn't a big deal.

"Yes we are. So tell me your side of the story Carmella," he stated while escorting her to his large living room.

Darletta viewed his beautiful home. She thought Carmella had great taste in men and Jackson was definitely a winner. Darletta sat down while Jackson went to pour her a drink. He returned with two flute glasses filled with club soda and lime. That was the drink he and Carmella enjoyed since neither of them indulged in alcohol. He handed Darletta the glass and sat down. Darletta sipped the drink and almost spit into the glass. She placed her hands to her lips wiping the corners of her mouth with her fingers.

In But A Moment

"What's wrong baby? Not enough lime or too much. I know I haven't lost my touch. I usually make your drink perfectly."

Darletta looked at Jackson and smiled. "No baby, it's perfect. The ice just hurt my teeth." She wanted to tell him give her a real drink with liquor. She forgot Carmella didn't drink or smoke. Having sex was just part of her plan.

"Hey, what's up? What you thinking about?" Jackson asked while watching Darletta.

He dreamed for so long to have her back with him. Then he thought back to the conversation he and Bill had. The nerve of Bill to assume or make up something about her sexuality. He knew better than anyone that Carmella was nowhere near gay. He always knew Bill really like Carmella, but he assumed it was purely innocent. But never in his wildest dreams would he ever believe that Bill would try to come on to Carmella. He also knew Carmella would not make something up like that. But what reason would Carmella have to lie?

Though he really wanted to make love to the woman he truly loved, he knew it would be to soon for that. She was hurting now and was probably having a hard time putting into words what Bill had done to her. He wanted to thank her yet tell her she didn't have to worry about he and Bill's friendship. He also knew that's why she made the story up about Jerome. She had a fear of jeopardizing he and Bill's friendship.

"Carmella," Jackson said. "Listen baby if it's too upsetting to discuss the situation we can discuss it at some other time okay?" He gently stroked the side of her face with the back of his hand and kissed her softly on her cheek. Then he looked into her eyes and the desire to want her grew stronger. Darletta smiled and turned her face to him and kissed his smooth lips.

14
<u>Changes</u>

The same nurse who led Nicole and Stacie to the waiting room earlier entered the room where the two ladies slept. The sun was shining brightly through the window despite the blinds being closed. The pretty nurse watched the two women while they slept, wishing she didn't have to disturb them. She had seen so many ugly incidents dealing with senseless killings, shooting, and victimization. She wanted to just touch the young women and tell them it was all just a terrible nightmare. But she knew that was not the case. What had happen was real. And she knew she had to wake the women to lead them to Dr. Bradshore who waited in his office to announce the condition of their friend.

Stacie slowly opened her eyes and could barely distinguish the silhouette that stood before her. She rubbed her eyes and looked around the unfamiliar surroundings. "What's going on?" she asked sitting up getting a clear view of the nurse assisting her.

"Hi, I'm nurse Robinson. Do you remember where you are and why?" she asked trying to help Stacie to gain her composure.

"I'm really not sure."

"You're at Presbyterian Hospital. This is where the paramedics brought your friend. Now do you remember?"

Stacie looked at the woman and then at her friend, who was still asleep.

"Yes I remember. Is Michelle okay?" she asked the nurse.

"I really don't have all the details, but I told Dr. Bradshore that I would bring you to his office, where he can explain everything to do.

"She didn't die did she?" Stacie asked as the whole horrible event danced in her head.

In But A Moment

"No, honey, she did not die, but I'm not at liberty to disclose any information to you. Dr. Brashore will explain everything. Let's go and see him. Do you want me to wake your friend or do you think it would be better for her to continue to sleep? You can go in and talk to the doctor."

"No, I'll get Nicole. She'll want to know what's going on." Stacie gently shook her friend. "Nicole, Nicole," she whispered. "Get up honey. We have to go see about Michelle."

Nicole woke up startled and confused. "How is Michelle?" she asked.

"I don't know, we have to go see her doctor. He's waiting for us now. Let's go."

Both Nicole and Stacie rose from the sofa and followed the nurse down the long brightly lit hall until they approached a large brass door that read in big gold letters across the top Dr. Robert Bradshore, MD. Nurse Robinson tapped lightly on the door and turned the knob before Dr. Bradshore had the opportunity to say come in.

The two women continued to follow Nurse Robinson into the office. It was a very spacious, comfortable office. Stacie looked around and saw brass framed pictures of very young children and a somewhat older gentleman, who favored the doctor. She focused on the neatly covered books lined on a wooden bookshelf. The office was handsome, as was the doctor who stood to greet them. Stacie watched his eyes intensely. There was something about him that brought warmth to her heart. She felt safe knowing that he was the one taking care of her friend. He had a simple gentleness about him that she liked.

He was a very tall man with very distinguished looks. He appeared to be a man who had great wisdom and confidence. She noticed he had a large dark black mole on the left side of his face towards his chin. It seemed to represent a sense of sexiness.

"Have a seat ladies," Dr. Bradshore announced as he led them toward two high back leather chairs sitting directly in front of his desk. "I'm Dr. Bradshore. I performed the operation on your friend Michelle."

"How is she Dr. Bradshore?" Nicole asked interrupting.

"Before I can disclose any information to the both of you, I need to know if Michelle has a family member that we can contact."

"No," Stacie announced.

She remembered the night Michelle finally told her of the relationship of she and her mother. She could look at Michelle and see all the hurt and pain she felt. She had gone through so much over the past three years of her life. Michelle left home at sixteen years of age for the streets for she had nowhere else to go. Her mother told her if she left not to come back. She would also tell her that she would never amount to anything Michelle. The hardest thing to swallow was when she said, "How dare you accuse my husband of molesting you? Go ahead leave Michelle. You've hurt your stepfather so bad he can't even look at you. I can't believe you would lie about him that way. You remember all the days left in your sorry life! If you walk out that door right now, you will walk out of our lives for good. To me you will be dead! You just remember that."

Michelle told Stacie how she ended up on the streets in the arms of Shakar Mills, better known as Big Daddy. He found Michelle and told her he'd take care of her. He would be her family. He took care of her all right; he forced her to work the streets for him as his girl. She did that for two years. Later someone had murdered Shakar and Michelle decided this was her chance to start over. She wanted a new start on life.

Her first attempt was to reconcile with her mother. She loved her mother, but her mother was not about to lose her chance for happiness in her life. She had found a man that loved her and her daughter. He was willing to take care of her and her child. He did just that, he cherished both mother and daughter. He was a good provider and gave Michelle everything in the world including the love she so desperately craved from her mother. She wanted her to love her so much.

The night Michelle left Robert William Garrett cried himself to sleep for he couldn't understand why the young woman he considered as his very own would tell her mother such a distorted lie. He had never touched Michelle and it broke his heart to think that she would accuse him of such an appalling act.

To him Michelle was everything he wanted in a daughter and he loved her in that way. He knew his wife did not treat Michelle the way a mother should treat her daughter and it disturbed him. So he expressed that to his wife.

Michelle called Barbara Jean Todds-Garrett on the 4th of July. When her mother answered and Michelle announced who she was she responded with coldness. "I don't know no Michelle. My daughter died two years ago." Then she hung up and never informed her husband of the telephone call.

That night Michelle tried to commit suicide by taking 100 tranquilizers. Her goal was to remove her from the pain and the hurt she had caused her stepfather and the loneliness of not having her mother's love. She knew she couldn't have asked for a better stepfather. She knew she hurt him more than he had ever been hurt and he did not deserve that. Michelle had nowhere to go, no family, no friends, and most of all she had lost her spirit for living.

When she woke she was in a Hospital with tubes running in and out of her body. She was in a state of depression that was too profound to achieve. She felt she couldn't even do that right. But, someone was happy she did not achieve what she had set out to do. The intern that sat by her bedside pulled Michelle threw and gave her a reason for living again. He spoke to Michelle everyday and night while she was hospitalized.

It was his way of giving back what he felt he missed with his own brother. When Michelle woke again, Michael James Morgan introduced himself. In her recovery they became friends. Michelle later explained to Michael what had happened. And she confided in him with the truth about her stepfather. They talked for many hours about her situation. When she was released from the hospital, Michael invited her to stay with him because she had nowhere else to go. Michael helped her land her first real job at Special Partnerships and helped her get her own place. When he knew she was going to be fine, he moved on with his life and followed in his Dad's footsteps and became Dr. Michael James Morgan, MD. His practice was located in Washington DC. Michelle promised she would stay in touch and she did. She was happy for him.

And now there she was again fighting for her life. Only this time it was not her fault. She was fighting to live now. Michelle had people in her life she considered her family and she knew they loved her.

Her friends, Stacie, Donna and Nicole loved her as their family too. Michelle had grown into a woman to be proud of and her friends were proud of her. They needed her to make it. After all Michelle had gone through, asking her to get in touch with the woman who totally despised her was crazy. She and her friends were Michelle's family now. Besides she didn't know how to get in touch with Barbara Jean if she wanted to. But she knew in her heart, it was the right thing to do.

"Do you know how to get in touch with Michelle's mother?"

"Michelle's mother does not live here. She is an only child and her father is deceased."

"Well do you happen to know of a way we can contact her mother? She should be here and be made aware of Michelle's condition. I'm sure she would like to know that her daughter has been injured and just got out of surgery."

In But A Moment

"Look Dr. Bradshore, no disrespect, but we don't know how to get in contact with Michelle's mother. She and Michelle have not spoken in many years. We are Michelle's family. Could you please just let us know what is going on with her? Is she going to be all right?" Stacie said while removing herself from the chair and leaning on the desk that Dr. Bradshore sat behind.

"Well, that's a hard question to answer. I'm sorry I didn't get your names."

"Oh I'm sorry. I'm Stacie Patterson and this is my girlfriend Nicole Grant."

"Well Ms. Patterson and Ms. Grant, we were able to remove the bullet from Michelle's head, but fluid has surrounded her brain. Therefore, we are not able to know what damage has taken place. We can't run test until the swelling has subsided. And until that time there really isn't too much we can do.

"But you got the bullet? That means she going to be okay, right?" Nicole asked watching the doctor very closely.

"Well Ms. Grant that's difficult to say. There is another problem here. Michelle slipped into a coma."

"Oh no!" Nicole cried. "Oh God, that means she could stay in a coma for years.

"Or it may just be one day," Dr. Bradshore said trying to shed some light to the situation. "You never know under these circumstances. We have to wait and see. She is going to need all the love and support you can give. That's why I thought it would be great if her family knew so they could be here for her. Sometimes the sound of familiar voices, her favorite song, or anything pleasing to her could help bring her back to us. It's going to be a very rough road for her and like I said we don't know what type of damage has occurred in her head. A lot of praying, support and love are what Michelle needs now. Can I count on the two of you for that?"

"Of course doctor! If it means we have to sit by her bedside everyday, we will do just that."

81

"Well, sitting with her everyday is not necessary, but as much as you can would be great. Talk to her just as if she were alert and well. And talk to her as much as you can. Nurse Robinson will explain in more detail about how to deal with Michelle's condition. Michelle has a rough fight ahead of her and she is not out of the woods yet."

Nicole continued to watch the doctor as the tears welled up in her eyes.

"Ms. Grant, I'm sorry I don't have better news for you, but like I said don't lose hope. Keep your faith and believe in your friend's recovery." Dr. Brashore walked over to Nicole to comfort her as Stacie watched the doctor knowing that her friend was going to make it.

"Thank you doctor," Stacie said while helping Nicole remove herself from the chair.

"Oh Ms. Patterson, if you can get in touch with Michelle's mother please do so. She has a right to know about her daughter's condition."

"I'll do my best, but I won't make any promises. May we see Michelle now please?" Stacie asked helping her friend to the door.

"Yes, Nurse Robinson will show you the way. I must warn you, Michelle is not going to look the way you expect her to. Her head is very, very swollen as well as her face, but eventually the swelling will go down. If either of you have any questions don't hesitate to contact me. Here's my card," he said while placing the card into Stacie's hand. "And please let me know if you've contacted her mother."

15
Mirror Image

"Good morning, Eunice," Bill stated in a slumber tone, while picking up the messages from his secretary's desk. He continued his walk into his office.

Eunice Thompson, looked up from her paperwork and watched Bill closely as she returned his greeting. "Good morning, Bill, how are you today?"

Usually he would stop and chat with her and tell her all about his past evening events. But, today was different he just wasn't himself. He couldn't get Carmella and Jackson out of his mind.

Mrs. Thompson looked perplexed as she watched Bill walk to his office. She knew Bill very well. He was more like a son rather than a boss. But that day he didn't seem like his old self. He seemed distant.

Bill walked over to the large window behind his desk and stared at the people running here and there trying to get to their given destinations. He wondered about his friend and even more about Carmella. The more he thought of how Carmella Springer had manipulated him, the more he wanted to find her and shake her to death. But it was pointless, she had already succeeded in tearing his heart out when she lied.

"That just doesn't sound like something Carmella would say or do, she just didn't appear to be herself. Why did she lie the way she did?" he asked. The ringing of the phone interrupted his thoughts. "Yes, this is Bill Tilmann."

"Oh hi Mr. Tilmann." An unfamiliar, but soft-spoken woman greeted him. "My name is Savassiea Smith and I'm calling from the North Hills office of Repeats. You are familiar with Repeats aren't you?"

Of course he was. It was where his ex-girlfriend Doris worked for years before she moved to California.

"Yes, I've heard of it," he said

"Well sir, the reason I'm calling is to see if you would be interested in having someone, preferably myself come and speak with you briefly to see if maybe we can help you gain some additional clientele. You see Mr. Tilmann, we've had our clientele for quite sometime and we are in the process of relocating to another area outside of Pittsburgh. Your organization was highly recommended by a personal friend. So I figured I'd give you a call to see if maybe we can give our clients over to you. Though we are leaving the area, we really didn't want to leave our clients hanging so to speak. Do you think this would be of an interest to you sir?"

Bill moved from the window and sat down in the large chair positioned behind his desk and smiled. "Why of course! It certainly would. When are you free to get together to go over the details?"

"Well, I can come to your office later this afternoon to discuss the details with you if your schedule permits."

"Yes, that's fine. Let's say around 2:15 PM?"

"Sounds great. If you would be so kind to give me directions I will see you at 2:15 PM."

"Sure, I'm located uptown on 5th Avenue. Are you familiar?"

"Yes I am."

"Great see you then."

Bill hung up the phone and smiled. Finally something good was about to happen to him. He wondered who this person was that recommended him. But, it really didn't matter, he was about to get more business.

Savassiea Smith hung up the phone and leaned back in her chair. She reached for a tissue standing so dutiful in the peach covering on her desk. Then she began to wipe the perspiration dancing on her forehead. Her heart was pounding and the same twitch that always appeared on the right side of her mouth when she was nervous began at the appropriate moment. She was very nervous and a little apprehensive on

In But A Moment

how and when she should do her dutiful promise. Being
docile was never a trait she was embarrassed of, but
sometimes it was a trait she could do without. After taking
couple of deep breaths she stood and began to place several
pieces of documentation into her briefcase. She proceeded to
go to her private bathroom and freshen up for her 2:15 PM
appointment. She viewed herself closely and was pleased
with the image that smiled back at her. For it was speaking to
her and saying you're doing the right thing. Once she felt she
was presentable she grabbed her briefcase and headed to the
office of Bill Tilmann praying that she was doing the right
thing. She was always good on her promises and she wasn't
about to turn her back on this one. In fact this was a promise
she knew not only in her mind she couldn't break. Besides
she wanted to know that the angel in heaven was singing a
joyful song.

16
<u>Stranger</u>

Darletta Springer positioned her body in such a way she was able to slowly view the strong dark body that laid beside her in the large brass bed. At first she didn't realize what had happened the previous night or where she was. Until she heard a groggy voice.

"Mm can I have some more?"

At that moment she realized what had happened. She had finally succeeded in what she was planning to do. She managed to hurt her twin sister just as she hurt her.

She sat up on the side of the bed and visualized the previous night. It was so easy with Jackson. Considering she hadn't made love with anyone since the incident she didn't think she would be able to do such a thing again in life. However, Jackson Waters changed that for her. He was so gentle with her that she could see why her sister was so very much in love with him. But it still did not excuse the fact that her sister didn't care about her when the horrible incident had happened to her. It was her life that got ruined in the process and Carmella was still complete as a woman. And she still had her dignity along with a man who really loved her.

She wondered if Jackson would hate her after finding about the game she just played on him. It was the only way to let her sister feel the hurt that she felt. She grabbed hold of the soft fluffy pillow and held it close to her chest. She sighed to herself, but she wasn't sure if it was a sigh of relief or confusion. Then she wondered if it was hurt about to happen all over again.

"Hey baby, are you hungry?"

If she could get rid of Jackson for a few minutes, it would be a good time for her to gather her thoughts,

"Oh yes baby, as a matter of fact I am starved," she said trying to loosen the grip Jackson had on her waist.

"Are you going to fix breakfast?" she asked, trying to sound congenial.

"Ah baby! I thought I could have a little more of you. That would satisfy my appetite," he told her smiling and watching her eyes.

"I know it would, my darling, but for real though, I am starving for food and maybe a little more of you when I'm done eating, okay?"

"Okay Spicy," he said kissing her. "Are you sure you don't want to join me in a shower? You know you always loved taking showers together," Jackson hollered from the bathroom while reaching to turn the shower knob on.

"No baby, you go ahead. I'll get mine later, okay?"

"All right. I'll get started on breakfast as soon as I'm done."

"Fine," she said looking bewildered. Darletta removed herself from the bed and walked out onto the patio. Although it was a little chilly, it did not affect the already frozen heart she had maintained for such a long time. At first she felt a little sorry for what had taken place, but soon the feeling of guilt subsided when she visualized the evil night that had changed her life. And she always felt her sister was relieved it her happened to her. All in one night her whole life had changed, she lost the love she held for her twin sister. She felt less of a woman. Her relationship towards men would never be the same again.

17
My Friend

Nurse Robinson lead the young women to where Michelle was. They would only be able to view her through the large window. Usually that was not even allowed, but since the doctor felt so badly for the young women he allowed the rule to be broken.

Nurse Robinson watched the women as they continued their walk down to room. The strong smell of medicine and cleaning products arrived at their nose as soon as Nurse Robinson opened the double doors.

Several times Stacie glanced at the nurse hoping she would sense her pain. As though reading her mind, Nurse Robinson placed her arm gently around the shoulder of Stacie and smiled at Nicole. "Don't worry ladies, Michelle's going to make it," she said with a pleasant smile. In her heart she was not sure of the statement she had just expressed to the young ladies. She wasn't sure what was going to happen. But she wanted to give them some type of hope. As the women got closer to the area tears welled up in their eyes. Nicole's hands began to sweat and shake as she grabbed onto Nurse Robinson's hand. The petite woman squeezed tight.

Once they arrived in front of the large window Nurse Robinson turned to both ladies. "I want you both to know that it's not going to be easy seeing your friend in this condition. However it is important that you also know that she is not feeling any pain right now. As Dr. Bradshore said, Michelle is not going to look like her old self, but with a lot of prayer and very skilled physicians as Dr. Bradshore, Michelle can and will pull through this. Okay?"

Nurse Robinson instructed the nurse behind the desk to please pull the blinds so the ladies could see their friend. When the woman behind the desk pulled the blinds, neither Stacie nor Nicole was prepared for what they saw.

In But A Moment

"Oh Michelle!" Nicole cried as she slid down the side of the wall and cried. Stacie tried to be strong for both her friends, but she felt herself beginning to fall apart as well. Michelle looked so contorted. She would have never imagined Michelle in the condition she was in. There were so many tubes running in and out of Michelle's body, you could barely see her. There were about six to seven machines in the small room. Her head and forehead were bandaged with heavy white gauze. And her face, what little you could see from the swelling, was severely bruised. Her beautiful hair was shaved off and her skin was dark, nothing like her pecan complexion she once had.

Stacie continued to view her friend through the window crying as she pressed her face against the steamy glass. "Oh God, please let my friends be okay. God, please help Michelle get through this and come out okay. And God, please help Nicole to be strong enough to hang in there. It's not fair!" she cried. "I know God, you are an able God. Therefore I know you know the desires of my heart. Dear Father in heaven, I pray that you will spare the life of both my friends. Dear Father, help me to hold on and be there for them for they need me more than ever right now. My Father, I need you more than ever. Please Dear Lord don't take her from me, not right now," she whispered. "Amen." She looked back at her friend and she felt as though her heart was slowly being removed from her body. Praying did not stop her from feeling the pain, but the restitution of knowing God was listening was satisfying to her.

She placed her hands against the window as if to send some type of vibe to her friend. Stacie continued to watch Michelle as Nurse Robinson helped Nicole off the floor. She told Stacie she was going to take Nicole to the lounge and give her something to help her calm down. "Thank you Nurse Robinson. I appreciate you being here for us. Nurse Robinson," Stacie called. "May I please go in? Please, I really want to be with Michelle," she begged.

The nurse walked over to Stacie and told her it was against the rules for right now.

"Nurse that is my very good friend in there, she doesn't have any family here other than us. Please, I know she is in a coma and maybe she won't hear me, but I want to at least try and let her know that the people who love her are praying for her. Please I am begging you!" As tears rolled down her face and her heart raced.

"Okay, Ms. Patterson, just for a minute. Go ahead."

"Thank you. Thank you so very much," she said and proceeded to push the door open.

She walked in and all she heard was the sound of machines appearing to be the life of Michelle now. She was once so vibrant and strong. Now she was so helpless and down. Stacie moved closer and touched the tip of Michelle's fingers.

"Michelle, it's Stacie, honey I want you to know that we are here for you and you're going to be okay. Don't you give up girl! We need you. You hang in there," she told her as she kissed her swollen cheek. The tears that now sprang from her eyes bounced onto the cheek of her friend. Michelle never moved, never blinked an eyelash. But Stacie knew she had heard her. And she knew that God had heard her prayers.

"Mom, I know you're here with me and Michelle. I don't know what to do. I don't want to loose Michelle. Mom, please help me. Let me know it's going to be okay."

And just as she said it a beautiful sparrow landed on the windowsill and flew off once Stacie saw it. Stacie knew it was a message her mother was trying to tell her.

18
<u>Vibes</u>

D onna watched David as he enjoyed the scrumptious breakfast she had just prepared. "Baby, I tell you your Mama sure did teach you well when it comes to cooking. You know that's the way to a man's heart right?"

"So they say," she said toying with the food on her plate.

David looked up from his plate and watched his girl. "Hey Babe, what's up? Are you okay?"

"Mm mm," she said knowing something was seriously wrong. She couldn't quite put her finger on what it was. She got up from the table removing her plate and walked towards the trashcan standing next to the sink and dumped the remaining food.

David glanced up at her once again. "Dang baby, you just wasted all that good food. You hardly touched a thing. Are you okay? You're not sick are you?"

"No baby I'm fine. You just go ahead and finish enjoying your breakfast," she told him. She just wasn't feeling well. The feeling she had passed over earlier that morning had returned and she wasn't sure what it was. All she knew was that it worried her. It was the same feeling she got when I grandmother was very sick and later she had died. She felt like God was trying to prepare her for the inevitable. "Honey, I think I'm going to wake Nicole up and see if she wants something to eat. After all I did make enough to feed an army." She smiled and kissed David on his bald head.

"Okay, that's cool baby."

She smiled and proceeded to walk towards Nicole's room but the sound of the phone stopped her.

"Hello?"

"Donna, it's Stacie."

Donna could hear in Stacie's voice something was wrong, and she immediately thought something had happened to her sister. Her face got hot and her heart began to race.

"Hi Stacie, is everything okay?" she asked in a whispered tone.

"Well not exactly are you sitting down? Is David still there with you?"

"Yes, Stacie please don't do this to me. Is it Nicole? Is she okay? Has something happened to Nicole?" Her voice began to skip. Now she was beginning to loose her patience. She wanted to know if her sister had been hurt and Stacie was taking too long to answer her questions.

Stacie knew how sensitive Donna was and she knew how close she and Nicole were with one another. Although the call was not pertaining to Nicole, she still felt it would hurt her. If she could see the state of mind her sister was in at that very moment it would break her heart. She always knew when something wasn't right with her sister.

"Donna no. It's not Nicole. Nicole is fine".

"Where are you Stacie? Hold on for a moment, she told her friend. And before Stacie could acknowledge what she had said, Donna threw the phone down and ran to Nicole's room. She opened the bedroom door and realized Nicole had never come home. The tears sprang to her eyes and she knew something was terribly wrong. That had explained why she was feeling the way she had felt earlier.

"Stacie where is Nicole? She's not in her room. Is she with you?"

"Yes Donna, Nicole is with me and she's fine. Donna it's Michelle."

"Mich? Oh God, please! What do you mean, it's Michelle?"

"Donna, Michelle has been shot." Stacie tried to be as calm as she could without allowing her true emotions to emerge.

"What?"

In But A Moment

"When you left the club. I noticed a really deranged looking guy talking to the woman we saw David with. At some point the woman must have pissed him off or he just got upset with her. Anyway he went off in the club on this woman." She continued to remain calm while speaking to Donna. But she could visualize the expression and position Donna was in at the very moment.

Donna sat down on the edge of the coffee table trying to focus in on everything Stacie was describing to her. "What does that have to do with Michelle?"

"Well apparently, he got pissed and began shooting onto the dance floor where Michelle was dancing and she got shot."

Donna placed her hand to her mouth and whispered. "How bad Stacie?"

"Donna, pretty bad. She was shot in the hea…."

"Oh God don't tell me she's dead, Stacie, please don't tell me she's dead. She began to cry openly.

David heard and leaped to her side. "Donna baby are you okay?" He got up from the table and ran to where she was. Her back was facing him.

"Donna she's not dead, she's in a coma. I will explain everything to you I'm on my way over there with Nicole to bring her home. Donna, Nicole's in pretty bad shape."

Donna placed her hand over her mouth to avoid the sound of pain. "Has Nicole been shot too?"

"No, Donna she's just very upset and she has taken it very badly. She really needs us honey."

"Okay, I'll be right there."

"No Donna, I'm coming to your place and I'll give you all the details. Wait there for me okay?"

"Okay," she told her and placed the phone back in its cradle.

David slowly walked up behind her and held her in his arms. "Baby is everything okay?" he whispered in her ear.

"No honey, it's Michelle. She's been shot David and oh God, how could this be happening? I don't understand," she cried turning to face him."

"Come here baby it's going to be okay." He led her to the sofa and sat down. Then he remembered she had gone to get her sister. "Where's Nicole Donna? Is she in her room?"

"No she's with Stacie. I assume they've been at the hospital all night. Stacie is on her way here with Nicole, will you stay with me?"

"Of course baby. Come here." He rocked her slowly in his arms. He wasn't really sure what had taken place. He wanted to ask how it happened, but he knew Donna wasn't in a condition to answer questions. Besides he wasn't sure she really knew the details.

Donna knew her sister was hurting the most. She wanted her there with her so she could hold her and let her know she was there for her. She began to pray while lying in David's arms. "God I love you on today, as I do each and every day of my life. Please Father, heal and protect both my sister and Michelle. God I don't know what all has happened, but I know you'll put it back in order." She began to cry as David continued to rub her back gently.

And that same feeling she felt earlier nestled again deep within her. She was glad David was there with her and that he could stay. She really needed him right now. For she knew her feelings were never wrong.

19
Strength

S tacie hung up the phone and stood for a moment in the phone booth trying to absorb everything that was happening. She walked out of the phone booth and began to search for Nurse Robinson.

"Nurse Robinson," she called out.

"Oh hello Miss Patterson."

"No, please call me Stacie. I just wanted to thank you again for being so understanding and patient with my friend and I. I truly am grateful."

"Well Miss Patterson, I mean Stacie, it's my pleasure. Anything I can do to help you let me know, okay?" She said touching her gently on her shoulder. "I've given Nicole a mild sedative, she should be waking up very shortly. Here." She handed her a small white piece of paper. "I've also given her a prescription to calm her down for a while okay? Please make sure she takes it to get filled okay?"

"Okay," Stacie told her reaching up and hugging her. "Take care of yourself and your friend Stacie. Here. These are the visiting times you are allowed to come and visit Michelle. Remember what Dr. Bradshore said, talk to her just as if she were sleeping okay? Only one person can go in at a time."

"Okay, I'm going to see if Nicole has waken up yet. And then I'm going to take her home. We'll be back sometime later today." She walked away as Nurse Robinson watched.

"Try and get some rest Stacie and don't forget to see if you can get in touch with Michelle's mother."

Stacie waved her hand in the air as she continued to walk away. She had no idea how to go about getting in touch with Michelle's mother. She also wondered if it was a good idea to even tell Michelle's mother.

She made a mental note to at least try and find a way to get in touch with Mrs. Todds. Like the doctor said, she did have a right to know, and it would be on Mrs. Todds to visit or show some type of interest in her daughter's well being. She was not going to carry a guilty feeling around within her.

"Hey sweetie!" she said gingerly to her friend.

Nicole sat up on the long sofa and smiled at her friend. "Hi back at you," she said.

"How are you feeling Nicole? The nurse told me she gave you something to help calm you down."

"Yeah, actually I'm feeling much better. How's Michelle?" she asked. Stacie watched her friend wanting to tell her it was all just a bad dream. But she knew the reality of what had happen.

"Well Michelle's condition has not changed Nicole. Nurse Robinson allowed me to go in to the room for a few minutes though. I spoke with Michelle. Nicole, I believe she heard me even though she didn't respond to what I was saying. I believe in my heart, she really did hear me."

"What did you say to her?" Nicole asked.

"I just told her that we all loved her very much and for her to get better because we all needed her. I let her know that we were here with her and that she was going to be okay."

"Oh," Nicole said looking perplexed. "Do you believe that Stacie?"

"Yes, to be honest with you Nicole I really do. Michelle is a strong woman and she'll fight to live. We just have to be strong for her and be here for her. That's all."

"I know, but I don't know if I can take Michelle looking the way she does and not knowing for sure she's going to be okay," she told her walking over towards the closet and getting her coat.

"I feel so terrible," she said looking in the small mirror beside the closet. "I need to go home and soak in a hot bubble bath."

In But A Moment

"Me too," Stacie said. "We both need a hot bubble bath and maybe a nap." She hugged her friend gently. "Oh yeah, Nurse Robinson gave this to me." She handed Nicole the small piece of paper Nurse Robinson had placed in her hand earlier. "She would like for you to get this filled and take one once a day for three days."

"Why? What is it?" she asked removing the paper from Stacie's hand.

"I believe it's a mild sedative. The same thing she gave you earlier to help you relax. You were in pretty bad shape Nicole. I would suggest you do has she says and take them. Remember you haven't gone in to see Michelle yet."

"Okay," she told her friend. "I'll get it filled." Then she pushed the button for the elevator.

The elevator door opened and both women entered. Stacie pushed the ground floor. "Oh I almost forgot," she said. "We rode over here in the ambulance, so we're going to have to catch a jitney back to the club to get Michelle's car."

Just the thought of having to go near that place made the hairs on Nicole's arms raise. Stacie looked over at her friend and she knew it was going to bother her to have to go back.

"Nicole, you stay here in the lobby. I'll go back to the club and pick up Michelle's car, okay?"

"Thank you Stacie. I'll wait right here for you."

"Okay, I'll be right back."

Arriving at the club seemed strange to Stacie. She glanced in the direction of where the ambulance had sat to carry her, Nicole and Michelle to the hospital. She felt a lump in her throat as she proceeded to walk towards Michelle's car. She didn't realize that the feeling getting into Michelle's car would affect her in such a peculiar way.

She opened the door and slid in. The faint smell of Michelle's favorite perfume lingered lightly over the steering wheel. Stacie placed her head down on the steering wheel to absorb the scent. She could feel the tears well up in her eyes.

Knowing she still had a small part of Michelle was indicative to her longing for her even more.

She traced the steering wheel with the palm of her hands and absorbed the scent of Michelle again. It left her feeling pleasant. The beauty of all she shared with Michelle flashed before her. There was a definite contrast of where she was and what she was about to go back to. And she wanted to stay where she was, allowing her to remember her as she was. She knew what she had just encountered was a glimpse of what was yet to come.

She started the engine and drove back to the hospital to get Nicole. When she arrived, Nicole was standing on the sidewalk. Nicole slid into the car and began to cry. Stacie turned and looked over at her friend and allowed her to grieve. She slowly placed her hand on her knee and told Nicole to let it out.

Nicole wiped her tears with the back of her hand. "Stacie, did you have a chance to call Donna?"

"Yes, Donna knows."

"How is she?"

"Well of course she's very upset and she's very worried about you. David is there with her. That's good."

"You know Stacie, it's so weird how things happen," she said to her friend laying her head back against the seat. "Michelle just wanted to have a good time. We all did. And now here she is fighting for her life. Her life will never be the same again, if she even makes it."

"Nicole, you have got to have faith that Michelle will make it and that's what we have to concentrate on!"

"Yeah, I know. But it's so hard to see that right now." She turned her head towards the window and noticed the beautiful colors painted on the trees. She loved fall it was her favorite time of year.

"I know it's hard, but we have to hold on too. Nicole, we have to be strong for Michelle now. Okay?"

"Okay," she told her. "But I hope I have enough strength to get to the level of strong."

"Don't worry if you don't I'm strong enough to pull you to the next level." She smiled and turned onto Coal Street.

Being strong for her friends was not a hard task because she had done it for so long. The challenge was contacting Mrs. Barbara Jean Todds. Her level of strength was about to be tested very soon. And she prayed that she wouldn't get weak.

20
<u>Going Home</u>

C armella threw the remaining articles of clothing in the large suitcase. She could barely keep her excitement contained. She was finally going home and she couldn't wait to see Jackson and be in his arms again. She only hoped her sister was able to pass the information she left on the answering machine on to him.

She had been trying for days to contact Darletta but always seemed to get the answering machine. She wanted to surprise Jackson with her return and hoped that he would be able to forgive her and love her once again.

"Well, somebody can't wait to get out of here!" a voice said from afar. It was her flight partner Charles smiling at her.

"That's right honey, I can't wait to get home and see…."

"I know your lover boy. But I thought you broke up before you left."

"Well that's a long story," she said concentrating on closing the large object on her bed. "All that matters now is that I'm going home and Jackson and I are going to be back together." She blew a sigh of relief. "Finished," she exclaimed finally accomplishing her task of packing. She had nearly two hours before her flight was scheduled to leave going back to Pittsburgh. And she knew it would be late when she arrived back home.

She visualized the welcome she would receive once Jackson saw her. A slow smile illuminated her face and the butterflies danced in her stomach like a high school youngster waiting for her date to arrive for the prom. She loved him so dearly and she couldn't wait to be in his arms again. The anticipation was exalting and the moment would soon be upon her. She sat on the edge of the bed and thought of all the many things she was going to say to Jackson once she saw him.

"Hey, girlfriend, I'm going to let you finish fantasizing about lover boy, cause I know that's what you're doing!" Charles said walking away and smiling in his heart. He loved Carmella and he hoped everything would work out for her. His advice to her was very reassuring at times when she really needed someone to talk to.

"Yoo hoo!" he said, peeking his head back in the door. "Did you hear what I said?"

"Sure did. But if I was fantasizing, do you really think I'd be listening to what you were saying?" she said smiling at him.

"Okay, point well taken. Be sweet, sweet drop." After that he vanished.

She smiled at her friend and removed the suitcase from the bed. Then she sat in front of the mirror adjacent to the bed. She took a long look at herself.

Carmella was a petite woman with a heart bigger than her whole frame. She began thinking very intensely about what was happening in her life and what was about to. She felt the tears well up in her eyes and finally hit the top of the porcelain dish that sat before her. She thought back to the incident that had happened with her sister. She had felt so guilty for so long and she had begged for her sister's forgiveness. And to this day she didn't know if she had it or not. In her heart she wasn't sure if she was the reason for the guilt she so often felt. She had tried everything to comfort her sister in her time of despair.

She could feel in her heart the uneasiness Darletta contrived whenever she was around. The love they had shared between them was far vanished. And she desperately wanted it back. She missed her and loved her so much. If only it had happened to her.

She took a deep breath and continued to view the image that sat before her. "Who am I really?" she asked

softly. But they were three powerful words that she didn't
know the answer to. She placed her small hands under her
defined chin and watched the single tear escape from her eye.
She wanted so much to be at peace and have everything back
the way it once was.

She wiped her eyes and walked over towards the
phone. She figured she would try to contact her twin one
more time. Three rings and the answering machine picked up
once again. "Darn!" she said. "Where in the world could that
girl be?" She knew Darletta didn't have any friends to get
together with. But she also knew that her sister could attract
people wherever she was. "But what in the world could she
possibly be doing all this time? She hoped nothing terrible
happened to her. Though she was an introvert, she had a way
of mouthing off when she shouldn't. Many times her mouth
got her in a whole heap of trouble.

She felt a sudden sting in the pit of her stomach that
left her with an uneasy feeling. Something was not right and
she was beginning to feel as though her sister was totally
involved. She picked up the phone and dialed Jackson's
number but then hung up and decided she'd rather see him
face to face.

Then she wondered if Darletta ever got any of her
messages, since all she had been getting was the answering
machine. But, how could that be? If she didn't have any
friends there, where could she be for such a long time?
Carmella tried calling her sister three or four times in the last
two days. Maybe Jackson never received the messages she
passed on to her sister. Or even worse maybe he got the
message and just didn't have it in his heart to forgive her. She
was confused and chagrined. For she was again permitting
her sister to fight her battles and again presuming the worse
scenario. It was her job to amend the situation between she
and Jackson and she was going to do just that.

She picked the phone up for the third time in the last
ten minutes and dialed Jackson Waters's number. "Come on

honey, be home! Be home honey, please." Her heart was pounding so fast she could see her tiny chest move.

"Hello?" There was a small pause and her heart escalated.

"Oh Jackson, thank…."

"This is Jackson. Sorry, I can't come to the phone. However, if you leave a number and a short message I'll return your call promptly."

"Man!" she screamed. "What is it with these answering machines? Does no one answer the phone anymore?" Then she remembered that Jackson at times screened his calls.   "Hello Jackson, it's Carmella. I know you're surprised to hear from me." She played with the cord on the phone and sat down on the edge of the bed as she continued speaking into the receiver. "I'm going to try and say as much as I can before your machine clicks off on me. I've been away on a trip. In fact I'm calling you from my hotel room. I'm due to come back to Pittsburgh early tomorrow morning." She smoothed the front of her skirt, trying to decide what she was going to say next. "I have so much to tell you. One thing I hope you can do is forgive me." She smiled imagining him sitting there listening to her voice over the answering machine. "I hope my sister had the opportunity to talk to you. I know you never met her and it probably was a shock when she introduced herself as my twin. Baby, I love…." She heard the final click indicating her announcement was at its limited. Immediately, she thought about calling back and completing her message but decided against it. Maybe it would be enough for him to absorb. And she had her fingers crossed that her sister had already talked to him.

Darletta smiled as she listened to her sister's disgraceful voice over the machine. She smiled as she hit the rewind button and then the erase button. After that she smiled and decided to join Jackson in the shower. She turned to walk towards the bathroom and Jackson stood before her looking at her with a mystified gaze.

21
<u>Loneliness</u>

S tacie pulled into the garage of her Forest Hills domain and sat for a minute before getting out of the vehicle.
She just wanted to relish the quiet moment. What she needed was a good night's sleep and she was thankful it was Saturday afternoon. Though she didn't like missing church, there was going to be an exception. Although she felt in the back of her mind she needed to go to church more than any other time in her life.

She was just so exhausted and burnt out both mentally and physically. She opened the door of her car and swung her legs out. Once inside, she immediately walked up the steps leading to her sunken living room. Her home was beautifully decorated, not by her, for she didn't have an ounce of creativity when it came to decorating. However, she had the final say so on what would be placed in her home. She loved black art therefore she made sure that beautiful black art was displayed throughout her home.

In addition to her love for black art she also loved Oriental furniture and objects. She had definitely done the right thing by hiring Sherean Mitchell, one of the best home interior decorators in Pittsburgh. And she was thankful she was able to hire her.

The Foyer was a pleasant introductory to the rest of Stacie's home. Large Graffiti chairs embedded the entrance with a flow of African sculptures artfully tucked on leather and chrome shelves. The scene left an intriguing blend and an eminently beautiful accent.

The living room was decorated softly and very feminine. It was painted in rich ivory, accented with gold boarding that sent a certain distinction throughout the room. The large bay window's nakedness was beautifully protected with shiny black Venetian blinds ornamented with puffed ivory valances nestled in their perfect places as tumbles of matching fabric cascaded down to the floor. Looking up at her bay window from outside one would see a handsome ivory, gold and black flower arrangement accented with birds of paradise, gold and ivory roses and a host of baby breaths sprayed gold and black.

The furniture of which she seldom sat was an Ivory Italian leather sectional containing six pieces. The rug of which it sat upon was a thick array of silken material that made it inviting to dismiss your shoes. Cappuccino walls and a glittered Japanese tea paper ceiling enhanced the already comfortable and nostalgic setting.

Overlaying a portion of the rug was a beautiful Mother of Pearl table with six matching stools. A top the table sat cleverly hand painted, detailed, porcelain Oriental women. She was proud of her Oriental women, for it was something her brother shipped to her for Christmas several years before when she purchased her home. It was more of a house-warming gift to her than a Christmas present. She treasured them, for she knew her brother really searched for the prefect gift for her and it touched her heart.

A large fireplace was snuggled at the base of the large wall from her bay window. Over her mantel place hung a beautiful oil painting of herself. Beautiful greenery cheered the room as well as a large Ficus tree hovering over the entire presence. A huge Mother of Pearl plant pot sat above the stairs that led to her living room. It was a beautiful piece of artwork that added grace to the room. Stacie loved items of beauty as well as quality. Her taste was very exquisite as well as expensive, but it had been that way since she was a young child. Money was not an object to her family and their motto was get what you will enjoy and love, because when you die you can't take any to Heaven with you.

Off from her living room, was the dining room, which sat a beautiful Mahogany eighteenth century styled English table with eight matching high back chairs. Sitting adjacent the table was a beautiful matching China Cabinet. Accolades of exquisite China dishes and glasses accentuated the cabinet. The table was decorated as though dinner guests were arriving at any moment. Pale pink cloth napkins judiciously sat on each plate designed with a handsome fan look. An intimate and beautifully decorated chandelier hung low introducing a soft glow over the decorative table.

A small kitchen decorated in sunny yellows anticipated smiles and happy moods. The yellow and white checked flood was so beautifully arranged it seemed unnatural to cover it. A large black refrigerator and matching stove clung to each side of the yellow and white checked cabinets. A long white breakfast bar and yellow stools produced the added touch to make the kitchen complete. The kitchen was positioned so that an abundance of sunlight invited itself in every morning.

There were two bedrooms in addition to Stacie's bedroom. The two guestrooms were handsomely decorated in hunter green and ivory. Stacie's bedroom was done in Mint Blue satin. Her Queen size four-poster bed was bejeweled with the cool material. The roman blinds accentuate the geometric windows while rolls blue satin materials kissed the top of each blind.

A mint blue net entwined a top her four-poster bed creating a soft silhouette. In the corner sat 25" color television. Next to her bed was a round table dressed with mint blue satin material. A top the glass tabletop sat her black cordless phone, leather phone book and fresh flowers. It always made her feel good to have fresh flowers everyday. There were two bathrooms as well as a powder room done in lilac. One bathroom was peach and white and other done in mint green and white.

The sitting room was Stacie's favorite room done in white soft leather captivated by Royal Blue walls trimmed in White. It was a bright room and always made her feel happy. A big screen TV sat along the corner of the wall while dozens of small and large framed pictures scattered the white shelves.

A stereo system sat along the opposite side of the wall with a host of CD displayed in their cases. It truly was a room that introduced comfort and cheer. And to this room she was headed. She entered and sat on the small leather sofa and reached for the small sliver framed picture above her head.

It started to rain outside. She listened tentatively as the drops of rain fell to their destination making a soft rhythm of their own. She always enjoyed the sound of raindrops. It made the house feel so serene. She traced the outside of the picture frame that caged her mother and father. She felt the tears well up in her eyes. She never realized how much she resembled her mother. Her mother was beautiful in every way to her and she smiled at the vision she saw before her. She had the same dimples and the same full mouth and perfect set of teeth as her mother.

She moved her eyes to the man standing next to her mother. Her father was a tall man and strong in every way. And she was his little girl. She wanted a man just like her father, someone who would protect and love her unconditionally. She had her father's same eyes, clear and focused. Her complexion was exactly like his, like honey. She pressed the picture to her chest and absorbed all of what she was feeling. She missed them both so much.

She knew her mother and father would be so proud of her. For they had raise her to be strong, independent and loving. She ached now of a desire she knew she couldn't have. She closed her eyes and laid her head on the arm of the sofa still clinging to her mother and father's picture.

She mediated for a moment. And when she opened her eyes she focused on the picture of her friends at last year's Christmas Eve party. They all were so happy. She wanted it all back the way it was. But she knew things had changed and she wondered if the happiness would ever return. She decided to take a hot bubble bath, throw on a CD and drink a glass of white cider while she bathed.

In But A Moment

Sinking into the water, she absorbed all there was to take. The pretty scent, the peacefulness, the sound of beautiful music, the raindrops kissing the windows of the bathroom and just loving her and who she was. She laid back and closed her eyes and the day's events somehow vanished. She knew in her heart loneliness was not going to be a best friend to her. It was just passing through and she greeted it and waved good-bye.

22
A Friend for Life

S avassiea Smith stood in front of the Professional
Building and smoothed her dress coat with the palm of
her hands. She glanced at her image in the glass window
before entering into the building. The image that smiled back
at her confirmed that she looked fine.

She looked smart with a gleam of elegance. She was
glad she went back to purchase the dress coat she thought
about all day after she left the store. She knew the dress
would come in handy. Her professional demeanor announced
that she was about business, yet she didn't come off too
powerful. She definitely was making a statement. She
glanced at her watch and knew that she had better get going.

She wasn't sure if she would really remember Bill
Tilmann and doubt that he would know her. She had seen
plenty of pictures of him, but never had the opportunity to
meet him in person. From what her friend had told her about
him, he was certainly someone worth meeting. Although she
didn't approve of what Doris and Bill's father decided to do,
she was not going to judge her friend. She respected her
decision, although she knew deep down Doris was still very
much in love with Bill. But the power Mr. Tilmann processed
over her was uncontrollable. It frighten her at times, how
Doris would let one individual have so much control over her
life. When she would try and mention it to Doris, she would
just tell her she loved Bill's father very much. And they both
felt bad it had to turn out this way, but they truly did love each
other very much.

Savassiea often wondered about that love, if maybe the
ugly green-eyed monster of money had a lot to do with it. As
she remembered Bill was still in college and working part
time, but that was not enough for Doris. She wanted someone
who could impress her with the materialistic things at that

very moment. Bill was not able to do that, though he loved her very much. Doris wanted something that Bill was not able to give her at that particular time. And she didn't have the patience to wait. While Bill studied and took classes during the summer, she was more and more inclined to quite evenings at home with Bill's dad, just talking and getting to know him.

Eventually, Bill's father grew to like Doris more than a soon to be daughter in-law. Soon she grew to love what Mr. Tilmann was able to do for her and that in turn forced her to love a man she truly didn't want. And in the interim she knew Bill would be devastated. It took her months before she found the courage to tell Bill what was going on.

And in the mean time she had to keep both men happy until she was able to break from one. She hoped in her heart that she would be able to turn from Bill's father. The amount of monetary pleasures he was able to provide always kept her at arm's length. It broke her heart when she saw the look in Bill's eyes when she announced what had been going on. But she had made a promise to herself and the woman about to meet Bill Tilmann.

And now was her opportunity to meet and greet him and tell him the most important thing he will ever hear in his whole entire life. Though she was a little nervous, she felt good knowing that she was the one that was able to put closure to the final chapter a lengthy book. If only Doris were around today to see the accomplishment this man had worked so hard to achieve.

If she had just a slim amount of patience, she would have had all the beautiful things she desired. But even more, she would be with a man she truly loved. But that was not near or there, for she was gone and Savanessia had a job to do now.

She entered the building and walked to the elevator. Once the door opened she entered and pressed her manicured finger against the number four on the elevator wall. She watched tentatively as the number lit announcing each floor.

Once arriving to the fourth floor she exited the elevator. She was surprised to see how colorful and handsomely decorated the reception area was. She allowed herself to assimilate the beauty of the area.

She then began to walk towards the distinguished looking woman seated behind the large white desk positioned in the middle of the floor. Eunice Thompson immediately raised her eyebrows towards the pretty young woman about to approach.

"Hello, may I help you?" she announced.

"Hello, my name is Savassiea Smith," she announced, extending her hand to Eunice. "I have an appointment with Mr. Tilmann." She wondered if that was the way she greeted all of Bill's appointments or was it just the way she was greeting her. It didn't matter. Nothing was going to get in the way of her divulging what needed to be divulged.

"One moment please," Eunice told her. She picked up the telephone and buzzed to Bill's office. In a very meek voice Savassiea heard Bill's receptionist announce his appointment.

Savassiea smiled when she heard Eunice tell Bill she wasn't aware of an appointment he had. She wished he would keep her abreast of such situations. She quietly hung the phone up and focused her attention back to Savassiea.

"Miss Smith, Mr. Tilmann will be right out. Won't you have a seat?" she said gesturing to the small round chair near her desk.

Savassiea followed Eunice's gesture and sat at the round chair near her desk. She couldn't help but notice the way Eunice continued to glance at her from behind the desk. To Savassiea it truly was unimportant. She was trying to concentrate on what words to say to Bill to help disclose the information she intended to tell him. She could feel her heart begin to pound and her palms begin to sweat and that darn twitch start to do its thing.

In But A Moment

Eunice just looked at her and wondered just what the woman was up to. Eunice usually had good instincts and from the instincts of which she felt, she knew the woman was perpetrating about something. But since the morning's beginning things were strange. Something wasn't right with her spirit. Something she felt in her heart was going to affect Bill. And she believed the pretty brown skinned woman sitting before her had something to do with it. Things were getting stranger by the minute.

It was unlike Bill to not inform her of a meeting. Maybe Ms. Smith was the reason Bill was so distant earlier. He certainly had been acting flustered and bizarre. Therefore why should this woman sitting before her stand for something out of the ordinary? She shook her head at her own thoughts and continued doing what she was doing before Savassiea entered the reception area. She lifted her head when she heard Bill's voice greeting Savassiea.

"Hello, Ms. Smith sorry to have kept you waiting," he said apologetically. He knew he didn't have a reason for keeping her waiting. He would have jumped through his skin if had he come out when she first arrived. He had to get his professional voice and disposition to its level of expertise before exiting out of his office.

"Oh no problem Mr. Tilmann. I was just basically getting acquainted with your lovely secretary. I'm sorry I didn't get your name," she said looking Eunice straight in the eyes. She knew Eunice could read through her.

Eunice Thompson looked up from her desk and duplicated the glare that Savassiea introduced to her. "Eunice Thompson," she announced in her penetrating, professional, vigorous voice. Then she returned her attention to the magazine.

Savassiea smiled and turned her attention to Bill. "Nice meeting you Eunice."

"Mrs. Thompson, thank you," she said watching the two of them walk away.

Bill gave Eunice a funny look and gently touched Savassiea's arm leading her towards his office. He knew Eunice could be harsh at times, especially if it was someone she didn't have positive vibes about. But he loved her all the same. She kept his company running smoothly and he was blessed to have found her. She was good people to him and he treated her as such. She was more like family. He didn't know why Eunice had such an odd air towards Savassiea. She seemed okay to him.

Savassiea didn't expect Bill to be so handsome. He looked much better than he did in the pictures she saw. She glanced at his hand to see if maybe he was wearing a ring. She smiled when she noticed there wasn't one. She could stare into his eyes forever. They were so beautiful. She could get totally absent in the beauty of his eyes. It was refreshing to look into them. She had never met an African American man who had such intense emerald color eyes before. And she knew they were not contacts, because his eyes were all Doris talked about.

"Please have a seat," he told her as he pulled out a large leather chair for her to sit upon.

"Thank you."

"So Miss Smith, let's hear what you have," Bill said while positioning himself on the corner of his desk.

Savassiea couldn't help but stare at the man before her. But she immediately put on her professional demeanor and presented a well-constructed presentation. "So you see Mr. Tilmann, that's what I like you to consider. This will give you the opportunity to gain new clientele and will give me the opportunity to move my business forward without leaving unsatisfied clienteles behind so to speak," she said while smiling. She knew he was impressed and knew he would agree to the arrangement.

Here she was extending a offer to him that only a cold-blooded fool would dismiss. Bill Tilmann was not that type of man. He knew when an great opportunity was upon him. The easy part was over as far as she was concerned. She knew he'd agree to the arrangements. It was part two that had her apprehensive.

She looked up into his emerald eyes. "So is it a deal?"

He returned her smiled and he knew he was going to like her though she was leaving Pittsburgh. But he could tell the way she carried herself and her sense of business abilities, she would leave him with the proper criteria and instructions to continue his business in a professional manner. He liked her business strategies and her style.

He looked her right in her eyes. "It's a deal." He held his hand out to her and she grabbed on and gave him a firm shake.

"You won't be disappointed, Mr. Tilmann I guarantee it."

"Please call me Bill."

"Okay Bill, you won't be disappointed," she said continuing to smile up at him. She was silently thinking about what she was going to say next to arrive at the subject she knew she was there to discuss. "Bill, I just have a few papers for you to sign off on and we can get the ball rolling."

"Fine, I'd like to take a look at them first and have my legal department view them as well. It's not that I don't trust you," he said warily.

"Why of course, by all means have your legal department view the documents and when you're ready to sign, I can either come back to your office or you can drop them in the mail. Which ever is more convenient for you."

"Well I was hoping you would stay, unless of course you have prior engagements."

"No, I don't. My afternoon is wide open. You were my only appointment this afternoon. The others are scheduled for tomorrow. I just didn't want you to think I was pushing you into something. You take all the time you need."

"Well, have you eaten lunch yet?"

"As a matter of fact I haven't."

"Good then I'll get my secretary to order us something and we can have lunch while the legal department is reviewing the documentation."

She thought that was perfect.

He liked her, and he wanted to get to know her better before she had to leave. She reminded him of someone but he couldn't put his finger on it. "Great! I'll get these to our legal department and ask Eunice to order some lunch and I'll be right back."

"Thank you," she whispered. She had no idea what to say to him or how to get him prepared for what she had to tell him. He was so jovial and she didn't have the heart to spoil his celebration. She figured she would wait it out a little. She wasn't leaving until the end of the month anyway. And besides she really liked him. And she could tell he liked her.

23
Image

W ho could that have been Jackson wondered from the bathroom. "Who was that?" he asked.

"Who honey?" Darletta said while walking back to the bathroom.

"Who was that on the phone?" he asked again.

"Oh that, that was some woman conducting some survey or something," she said waving her hand in the air.

"Oh that always bothered me."

"What?" she yelled back at him.

"How you have to pay to have an unlisted number, yet everyone in God's creation has access to it. What's wrong with this picture?" he asked in a playful tone. "I just don't get it," he said catching up to her and grabbing her around the waist from behind. "Come on baby, let's skip breakfast and go back to bed."

He was really beginning to get on her nerves. She didn't have time to participate in his silly games. She had to get to that airport to catch her sister before she had the opportunity to catch Jackson. "No, come on Jackson!" she said pushing his hands away from her. "I have something I need to take care of today. I'll tell you what, if you're a good boy, Mommy will bring you something delicious to eat back," she said patting him on the head and pretending to play his simple game.

"Well can't I just taste a little right now?"

"No, see you're trying to misbehave."

He loved when she teased him. Darletta saw that he was getting a kick out of her teasing. It must have been something Carmella constantly did to him. To her he looked stupid pretending to be a kid. He needed to grow up. She had other serious plans to concentrate on, although the idea of hopping back into bed with him wasn't a bad request. In fact, she looked forward to many more opportunities. He was a great lover. But her game wasn't about making continuous love. She succeeded in what she needed to do. Now she had to get to her sister and he was prolonging her ability of doing that. She had to think quickly. She didn't expect Carmella home so quickly.

She faced Jackson and touched his lips with her fingers. "No seriously Jackson, don't you have to get to work? I really do have something I need to take care of today."

"All right, I'm getting dressed."

"Baby I'll see you tonight. Let's have a late night dinner by candlelight okay?" she announced from the bathroom.

"Okay, baby, you have a good day and I'll see you tonight."

She shut the bathroom door and stepped into the shower he left running.

Jackson finished dressing and was tempted to rewind the tape on the answering machine, but decided against it. Carmella had no reason to lie to him. Even though he felt as though something just wasn't right, he could feel it in his soul. He'd let it pass. He felt good today and no one was going to break his spirit.

Darletta dressed and was out the door not too long after Jackson. As she left, the phone rang again.

"Jackson, where are you? It's me Carmella. I'm back in Pittsburgh. I was expecting to see you at the Airport. I miss you. Well, I guess I'll see you later."

Darletta was determined to meet her sister at the Airport before she was able to contact Jackson. Though she had succeeded with her plan, for a split second she felt a seed of guilt. But she got over it quickly. She knew the truth was going to come out sooner or later, but she preferred later. She had to think exactly what it was she was going to say to her sister to disclose what she had done with Jackson without

Carmella getting too upset. But there was no denying it, she was going to be furious and devastated. What she wanted her to feel was the same hurtful feelings she experienced. But, she was prepared. She didn't want to have to disclose anything right now. And she didn't want Carmella to be so upset, for fear of her disclosing anything to Jackson.

She wasn't ready for that to happen, and besides her sister had made a promise to her. She believed she'd keep that promise no matter what. Sometimes secretly she wished they were back to the way they use to be. She just couldn't go back to the way she was with her sister. She wanted Carmella to feel the same pain she was feeling after all they were twins. There was no easy way to tell her she had slept with her boyfriend. So she was just going to have to come straight out and say it. She knew her little game couldn't last forever. She wasn't regretful for what she had done, why should she be? No one was regretful for what happened to her. For she was the one feeling infirmity, for something that should have never happened to her.

She was glad she had gotten to all three of them, Carmella, Jackson and Bill. She wasn't about to give up on the final move in her game.

"Man, I forgot the last pages of my presentation on that desk," Jackson said. Realizing after entering onto the Parkway. He spun around and headed back home.

He entered through the garage and ran up the steps. Once inside he hurried towards his office and grabbed the three pages of his presentation sitting exactly where he had left them. He walked back towards the kitchen while looking over the final three pages of his presentation. He smiled for he knew his presentation was going to be excellent. He worked very hard, and he knew it was about to pay off. For this was the presentation that was going to show his true colors and just what he was capable of doing.

This time, Mr. Woodson was not going to be able to take the credit for his work. He had researched a new product, a product that Mr. Woodson was not familiar with. This was going to be the break he was looking for and he was going to love watching Mr. Woodson's face.

He walked towards the refrigerator and reached for the orange juice sitting on the side. Continuing to glance at his papers, he reached for a glass and poured himself a tall glass. He noticed the red light blinking on his answering machine. So he walked over towards the machine and pressed the play button.

"Jackson, where are you? It's me Carmella. I'm back in Pittsburgh. I was expecting to see you at the Airport. I miss you. Well, I guess I'll see you later."

He replayed the message, sat the glass of juice down and listened. Each time the message repeated itself he stood looking perplexed. "What the hell is going on? Camella?" He sat on the counter stool and listened to the message several more times before realizing it really was Carmella. He picked up the phone and called Mr. Woodson's office.

"Good Morning, Mr. Woodson's office may I help you?"

"Yes, good morning, Carla, this is Jackson Waters. Could you please let Mr. Woodson know I'm going to be late this morning? An emergency has come up. I'll be there in plenty of time for the presentation today at 2:00 PM." He wasn't about to miss the opportunity of watching Mr. Woodson squirm.

"Is everything okay Jackson?"

"Yes. It will be. Thanks a lot," he said as he hung up. He knew something wasn't right, he could feel it. And he was determined to find out what it was. Then he instantly thought back to the night at Bill's Condo. Maybe Bill was telling the truth. Maybe the Carmella we think is Carmella really isn't. He rubbed his temples and remained confused. Why in the world would Carmella be calling him when he had just left her this morning? He leaned over the countertop. If that was Carmella on the phone, then who in the hell was that he slept with last night and talked with this morning.

He picked up the phone one more time and dialed Bill's office.

"Good morning Mr. Tilmann's office, may I help you?"

"Good morning Eunice. This is Jackson. Is Bill available?"

"Oh hello Jackson, how are you?"

"Just fine thank you. Is Bill around?" He knew he sounded anxious, but he really needed to talk to Bill. He didn't have time to chitchat with Eunice at that moment.

"Yes, hold on. I'll put you through." She hit the flash button and dialed Bill's extension.

"Bill Tilmann."

"Bill, hey man it's Jackson." Jackson knew Bill would be shocked to hear from him or even accept his call.

"Jackson, well this certainly is a surprise to hear from you. What's up? Is everything okay?"

The evening at his condo flashed in his mind and soon vanished. Jackson sounded strange to him. He thought that maybe he was in some type of trouble. He didn't care what had happened between the two of them. If Jackson was calling him something was definitely wrong.

"No, I need you to come to the Pittsburgh International Airport with me."

"When?"

"Right now. Can you get away?"

"Sure, no problem."

"Good I'll meet you outside your building in about 20 minutes."

"Jackson, what's going on?"

"I'll explain everything when I see you."

Bill hung up the phone and wondered what was happening. First a strange visit from a woman, offering him business, and now a call from Jackson. He felt he'd never hear from him again. Something was wrong and he knew it had something to do with Carmella Springer. Whatever it was he was willing to put all differences aside and help Jackson. He grabbed his suit jacket.

"Eunice, I'll be back in about two hours or so. Please take all my calls." He walked towards the elevator and pushed the button. "Oh yeah, if Ms. Smith calls please get a number where I can reach her."

Eunice watched as Bill entered the elevator. "Now just what is going on here?" she whispered. "Okay Bill," she hollered after him. Then she sat at her desk with her hands fixed under her chin and wondered as she shook her head. "Well it ain't none of my business anyway," she said out loud. But she was going to find out what happened. Nothing got past Eunice Thompson, nothing.

24
Sisters and Brothers

J ackson pulled along side the curb outside of the Professional Building. Bill saw Jackson as soon as he stepped out of the building. It was perfect timing. After giving Eunice the necessary details he stopped at the legal department to find out the status of the documents he left yesterday. Everything was complete and satisfactory. He made a mental note to call Savassiea when he finished his business with Jackson.

He climbed into his friend's car and wondered what was going on with him. There was an awkward silence between both men. Not sure what to say, Bill reached over and shook Jackson's hand with a bona fide brothers shake. Jackson watched him and smiled. He was glad they were back to being friends. There was no need to discuss the confusion that had taken place between them. To Bill it was all in the past and he understood where Jackson was with him mentally. It was all done with.

What was important was that they both were back as being brothers rather than just friends. Bill knew his friend needed him and he knew if he had some sort of trouble, Jackson would be there for him too.

"So, how's Carmella, Jackson?" He didn't intend to bring Carmella's name up. Somehow the words just escaped his mouth. He watched his friend and tried to figure out if mentioning Carmella's name was a good idea.

Jackson had no problem discussing Carmella for that was the mission he was about to take Bill on.

"That's what this ride is all about Bill. I'm not sure what's going, but I don't think the woman that you and I both came in contact with is who she says she is."

Bill looked at his friend and grew confused by what he was telling him. But if it were true that explained why

Carmella was not acting the way he was used to seeing her. He knew there was something artificial about the woman who had caused all kinds of friction between he and his friend.

"What are you talking about Jackson?"

"What I'm saying is the woman we think is Carmella Springer is not Carmella Springer." He turned and glanced at this friend, who was sitting with a bewildered look on his face. "Okay listen, I went back to the house this morning for something and Carmella or whatever her name is had gone. She had told me she had something to do today. Anyway I go home and notice my answering machine light is blinking. So I check the message. And there's a message from Carmella saying something about she thought I was coming to the airport to pick her up."

"What?" Bill said listening intensely.

"Yeah, exactly! So I figure whoever this woman is knows that Carmella is at the airport, therefore she's going there to meet her."

"But, I mean Jackson, they look exactly alike, how could it not be Carmella. Have you ever met anyone in her family?"

"I've never met anyone in Carmella's family, but I believe it's Carmella's twin sister. It has to be."

"That would explain a great deal," Bill said.

"Well I figured we go check it out for ourselves."

"I'm game!" Bill said knowing it would ease his mind that it wasn't all his imagination.

Jackson could feel the anticipation grow stronger as he got closer to the airport. He couldn't wait to approach whoever it was portraying to be Carmella. He also couldn't wait to approach Carmella so she could explain everything. Despite what was going to happen he never stopped loving her. And in his heart he wanted to see her.

"Man, this whole week has been strange for me too."

"How so?"

"Well, I get this mysterious call from a woman named Savassiea Smith."

"Beautiful name," Jackson added

"Beautiful woman," Bill confirmed

"Oh boy, watch out Ms. Smith! He's on a roll," Jackson stated glancing at his friend.

"Well, I do like her, but she's different from any other woman I've met."

"Yeah, I've heard that one before."

"No, seriously I really like her, although it doesn't matter. She's going back to California at the end of the month."

"Maybe you can change her mind," Jackson told his friend.

"I doubt it, her heart and mind are set. The purpose for us even meeting was for her to introduce me to a business proposition, which I have accepted. So therefore there will be no need for us to see each other again."

"Ah come Bill, since when have you let go of a challenge? Just go for it."

Bill smiled, for he had all intentions on going for it. He really liked her. He was going to call her and ask her out to dinner later. That way he could give her the documents she needed to close the deal.

"You're right, I can't let go of a challenge," both men laughed.

Jackson pulled into the parking garage of Pittsburgh International Airport. "Are you ready?" he asked Bill.

"Let's do this."

Carmella stood at baggage claims waiting patiently for her suitcase to slide down the conveyer belt when she heard her name being called over the loud speaker. "Carmella Springer please report to the information desk." Immediately, she smiled thinking Jackson had come after all. She rushed to information and saw her sister waiting patiently for her.

"Hey? Hi." She hugged her sister. "Where's Jackson?"

"Oh he couldn't make it. He couldn't get out of work, so I came." She watched Carmella's expression confirming she was disappointed Jackson did not come along.

"He does know I'm home now, doesn't he?" Suspiciously, she watched Darletta. You did have an opportunity to tell him everything didn't you Darletta?"

"Yes, I did. Come on let's go get your things and go home." She placed her arm around her sister's shoulder.

Carmella didn't believe her and she knew her sister was up to something. She was appearing to be too nice and considerate with her.

"Hurry up Carmella!" Darletta insisted

"What's the hurry Darletta?"

Carmella and Darletta continued to the escalators leading to the baggage claim. Darletta continued to talk to Carmella trying to take her mind off Jackson. But it was too late. When both women got to the end of the escalator, Jackson and Bill were there to greet them.

"Well I'll be!" Jackson stated as he looked at both women.

Bill never stopped looking at them for he couldn't believe how one would portray another. What could possibly cause her to do that? And what would cause her to want to hurt her sister as she did? He thought she was demented.

"Hi Jackson!" Carmella looked at him feeling all the love she had inside her build up by just watching him. "I thought maybe you didn't get my message," she said softly as she continued to watch him. She wanted so bad to run over to him. Then she focused her attention to Bill. "Hello Bill, how are you?"

"What's up?" They were the only words he could say.

"Yes I'm sure someone intended for me not to get your message or should I say messages?" He glanced at Darletta.

126

In But A Moment

"So I bet it surprised you to find out I had a twin sister, huh?"

They all continued walking towards the baggage claim area.

Jackson ignored her question. "Carmella we have got to talk!"

Carmella looked into his eyes and she knew her feelings were right about Darletta. She knew something had happened, something that would not be pleasing to either of them.

Jackson grabbed Carmella by the hand and led her to the first set of seats he could find. Darletta tried to continue walking but Bill gently pulled her to a seat.

"Now, should I tell everything that happened or should you Ms. Darletta?"

"What happened Darletta?" Carmella asked with fear.

"Let me say this to you Carmella. If you ever disclose what happened to me, I'll never forgive you for as long as I live!" She looked her directly in her eyes. She could see the pain she so desperately wanted her sister to feel. She was hurt and she wanted her sister to feel the same hurt.

"I would never do that Darletta. I made a promise to you."

Darletta glanced at Jackson and Bill. She knew she had done some heavy damage. She thought she was able to separate all of them. Her sister had won again and she hated her for it.

"What happened?" Carmella said throwing her hands in the air.

"You want to know? Then let me tell it."

"Shut up Darletta! I will tell what has been going on," Jackson announced. "See I've got your number Darletta. Now you want to be so audible. Well I'm the one in control here. Okay? So just shut up and listen!"

"Cut the bull Jackson! You and I slept together. And that's all that's to it. Why you got to get all emotional and serene about it? Just say it! We slept together. What's so hard about it? Why does it take so much thought? Oh, or maybe you were trying to protect poor Carmella. Please my brother, get a grip!" She positioned herself to leave the seat she was sitting.

Bill placed a tight grip on her arm and almost threw her back down in the chair. She was such a witch he thought. It was like she and Carmella were not related. He couldn't believe what she just did. He looked at Carmella as tears filled her eyes.

"You did what?" Carmella moved towards her sister and began to cry. "Darletta, how could you?"

"Hey it just happened."

"Excuse me," Jackson butted in. "I don't think it just happened. Tell the truth! You pretended to be Carmella all this time. You fooled Bill and me. I thought...." He looked back at Carmella. "I thought it was you coming to me asking for my forgiveness. I accepted and we were a couple again. In the meantime she had tried to destroy me and Bill's friendship."

"How?" Carmella asked, watching her sister.

"She went over to Bill's place and told him some lie about you being gay."

"When I arrived at Bill's place I saw your car and assumed you were with Bill. Then she re-entered and told me that Bill was trying to come on to her."

"Oh my God, Darletta, how could you?"

"I believed her." He looked at Bill and shook his head.

Carmella looked at her sister and she knew what it meant to be portrayed. She watched Darletta and knew that it was true.

Darletta looked at her sister and for the first time tears sprang from her eyes. "I hate you!" She said the words with such force it frightened Carmella.

In But A Moment

"Darletta, were you protected when you and Jackson had sex?" She moved closer to her. Jackson lifted his head and looked at both Carmella and Darletta.

Darletta smiled and watched Jackson's face. "No, thanks to you I didn't have time to ask. You and Jackson never used protection."

"Don't you think he deserved that Darletta? What kind of sick game are you playing with people's lives? Damn you!" For the first time she wanted to slap her sister and she came very close to doing just that. Jackson stopped her. "You didn't care what game you were playing with me, did you? As long as it was me." She began to cry again. "I did the suffering. Nothing happened to you." Carmella was shaking and out of control, she could not believe her sister would go that low as to involve innocent people in a horrid game of life or death.

"When are you going to get it Darletta?" She fell to her knees and cried as she pounded her chest. "I'm not the one to blame for your rape."

Darletta slapped her across her face as hard as she could. "You witch!" she screamed. "I hate you!" Suddenly, she charged after her. Bill and Jackson grabbed her and threw her in the chair.

"I'm sorry. I'm sorry." She grabbed on to her sister's arm. She didn't mean to blurt out the secret.

Darletta looked at her and got up out of her chair and walked away.

"Rape?" Jackson lifted Carmella up from the floor and held her in his arms. "What are you talking about Carmella? Talk to me."

"I can't Jackson. I'm sorry."

"Carmella, this is ridiculously! What the hell is happening?"

She knew he deserved to know since he was completely involved. And it was her fault he was in the situation. She sat back down and explained the whole story to

129

both Jackson and Bill. It didn't matter now about the secret, too many people were involved now. She should have told someone a long time ago. Darletta would have had help by now. Maybe she would be ready to enjoy life again.

She told them how Jerome Lockhart had mistaken her sister Darletta as her when she was walking back from the corner store late one evening. Usually she would have driven, but because it was so nice that night she decided to take the walk. Jerome saw her thinking she was Carmella.

He was upset because she had broken it off with him. The more Darletta said she was not Carmella the more he didn't believe her. He dragged her back to his car and raped her and threw her out of the car into the back alley one block from the store. Because she had taken so long to come back from the store, Carmella had rode to the store to pick her up. She found her lying on the ground in the back alley. She rushed her to the emergency room and called the police.

After having the necessary tests run on her. Carmella gave the Police report after taking Darletta home. Several days later the hospital called and asked the both of them to come in. It was later disclosed to Darletta that she had tested HIV positive. At first she didn't believe what the doctor had just disclosed to her. She was in denial for weeks. She then went and had another test. It came back positive again. Several weeks later Jerome died from AIDS. Carmella went for testing too. Her test came back negative. She had only slept with Jerome once during their relationship. He was very abusive towards her. Once Darletta found out Carmella tested negative, she despised her and blamed her for her mishap. The hospital offered her counseling but she refused. She's been living with the pain all this time.

Jackson looked at her and tears welled up in his eyes. "Are you telling me your sister has AIDS?"

"Jackson, I'm so sorry, I never meant for any of this to happen."

"Wait! Are you telling me your sister has AIDS?"

In But A Moment

"No, Jackson I'm not saying that. I'm saying she has been diagnosed as HIV positive."

"I don't believe this! That witch!" He paced the small area. He sat down and placed his head in his hands.

Carmella was so sorry, she didn't mean to hurt him this way. She walked towards him and held him as he cried. He had no idea if he was infected.

"Jackson, the first thing we need to do is get you tested."

He removed her hands from him. "We? I don't think there is a we!" he said swinging his fingers in her face. He wanted to love her but this was just too much for him to handle. He got up and walked out the door. Bill followed.

Carmella stood alone in the doorway watching the man she loved walk right out of her life. And she knew her sister had received her wish. She walked over to claims, picked up her bags and headed for the first Cab she saw outside. She slid in and cried for her sister and the man she would love forever.

No matter what her sister was, she still was her sister, and though she had done terrible things she still loved her. She didn't understand what was happening. It took just little time for everything to change.

25
<u>Tears</u>

Nicole tossed and turned for hours before getting out of her king sized bed. She just wasn't in the mood for sleeping. Besides she had done so much of it since Michelle's dreadful ordeal. One month had passed and Michelle had not come out of the coma. She and her sister as well as Stacie had gone to the hospital everyday to sit with Michelle and just talk to her about the days events happening in each of their lives. They all missed her and wanted her to her old self again.

Dr. Bradshore was right when he told them it could be a long process. Though they were not completely used to Michelle lying up in a coma, they were used to the rearranging of their schedules to be sure someone was with Michelle. Just in case she would come out of it.

No one had even attempted to contact Michelle's mother. The thought just made everyone feel too down. Though Dr. Bradshore was asking every chance he got, no one was keen about performing the task of trying to contact her. And no one was really sure that's what Michelle needed.

Tonight, however, was different. Nicole thought maybe if Michelle's mother were to know about Michelle's condition she would finally come to her daughter's side. And just maybe Michelle could come out of the coma. Wishful thinking she thought to herself. But, she was at the point of trying anything if it would aid in Michelle's complete recovery.   It was 1:45 AM and there she was sitting up like it was in the afternoon. She knew both Donna and Stacie would be in a deep sleep. Besides she didn't have the heart to wake either them. She did have the key to Michelle's apartment. They each took turns checking on her apartment.

She ran to the bathroom, washed her face, brushed her teeth and pulled her braids back off her face. Then she ran back to her room being careful not to wake her sister. David had left earlier that day for a business trip. He was a real comfort to both she and Donna. Nicole threw on her jeans and an oversized sweatshirt. She grabbed her coat and out the door she went.

The night air was cold against her face and the frozen raindrops were a sure sign that winter was near. She hated Pittsburgh winters. They were entirely too cold in her opinion. And when it snowed, it really snowed. Summer was her season. She looked up at the sky. It was clear and beautiful. What a beautiful night for miracles to happen, she thought.

She smiled and slid into her car and started the ignition. She wasn't sure what she would say or do if she was able to contact Mrs. Todds. She would worry about that when the time came. Right now she was concentrating on getting to Michelle's apartment and finding what she needed to find.

In less than thirty minutes she was sitting outside of Michelle's apartment. The neighborhood was quiet and peaceful and she was grateful. She rushed into Michelle's apartment and saw that everything seemed to be in order. Donna had done a nice job last week making sure everything was spotless.

Nicole continued to Michelle's bedroom, but she stopped for a minute before proceeding into the room. She never realized entering into Michelle's apartment would make her feel so sad still. She could feel her presence all over the apartment. It was almost as if Michelle were right there in her room laughing on the phone and telling her to come on back.

She had to remove the sad thoughts from her mind because she had more important things to think about. She sat on the side of the large bed and picked up the little black phone book sitting on the nightstand. "Let's see." She began flipping through the pages. "Thompson, Tilmann, Tnods, Todds." She traced her finger on the letters. "Todds," she whispered. "This has to be her mother's number." She picked up the phone and quickly placed it back in its cradle. "I must be out of my mind. It's 2:30 in the morning. They'll probably think I'm some crank caller or something." She sat back on the bed and thought about what she would say.

The ringing of the phone startled her. "Now, who in their right mind would be calling someone's house this time of morning?" Then she smiled to herself because she was just about to do the same thing. At first she hesitated before answering the phone. Maybe it was just a wrong number. Or maybe it was someone who had been trying to contact Michelle. Or maybe it was her mother following her intuition of her child in trouble. She stared at the framed picture on Michelle's nightstand, which was no doubt a picture of her mother. Michelle resembled her a great deal. She smiled and yet felt like crying. Despite everything that Michelle's mother had done she knew Michelle still loved her very much.

"Hello?" she said while placing the phone under her chin for support.

"Well, hello. I've only been trying to get in touch with you for the past week now. I think it's a shame to have to call you this time of morning, but I figured I'd get you. And I see I was right," the strong deep voice on the other end stated.

"I'm sorry?"

"Oh, I'm sorry. I'm trying to reach Michelle. Michelle Todds. Maybe I've dialed the wrong number. I'm sorry."

"No wait! Don't hang up. You have the right number. My name is Nicole, Nicole Grant," she stated. "Who I'm I speaking to?"

"Michael Morgan," he told her. "Where is Michelle?" "I'm sorry Michael, I don't remember Michelle ever mentioning you to me. Are you a good friend of Michelle?"

Michael was beginning to worry. Something in the young lady's voice didn't sound right and he was afraid for his friend. "Look Nicole, I am a very good friend of Michelle's. I live in California, and she knows me very well. I have been trying to get in touch with her for the past three weeks. Has something happened to her? Is she there?" He could feel himself beginning to loose patience with Nicole.

"No Michelle is not here."

"Well do you happen to know where she is?"

"Yes, Michael" she said trying to prepare him for what she was about to say. "I'm sorry Michael, Michelle has been in an accident."

"What?" He felt his heart race. What kind of accident?"

"She's been shot."

"Shot? Wait a minute, how was she shot? Where is she?"

Nicole knew the information she just disclosed had upset him. "Michael?" There was silence but she thought she heard a soft whimper. "Michael, I'm very sorry." She wanted him to know that she knew what he was feeling, though she had never met him. "Michael, I want you to know that Michelle is a fighter. I believe she is going to make it. We have to encourage her to hang in there."

"Where is she? How bad was she shot?" He could tell from Nicole's voice, Michelle was not completely out of the woods. "When did this happen?"

He sat down behind the desk in the small room he had converted into his office. This would explain why he was feeling so down lately. He was worried about Michelle. It was not like her to not keep in touch with him. He had been trying to get in touch with her to tell her what had been happening to him.

He wanted to tell her that he was in love with her and that he and his wife had divorced. He hadn't mentioned the divorce thing to her for fear of it not happening. But, his ex was very cooperative. She knew he did not love her and it was because of the birth of their daughter he stayed with her. She agreed to the arrangements he had disclosed.

Shérri A. Gambrill

She told him he could have full custody of their daughter as long as she got to have her every summer. Though she loved her daughter, she knew he was a much better parent. They had agreed they would remain friends for the sake of their daughter.

And he wanted to share the news with the woman he loved. What was wrong with this picture? Right when everything was going so well, the closing piece for the puzzle was totally out of position. He loved her the first time he set eyes on her in the hospital when she tried to end her life. He knew his only reason for marrying Elese was because she was carrying his baby and he felt it was the right thing to do at the time. He thought he could love Elese and in a sense he did, but not the way a husband and wife should love one another

It was Michelle he always had true love for. He thought about her everyday. He could be himself with her. He wondered if it was too late.

"It's been about one month since the accident Michael," Nicole said interrupting his thoughts. "There's one more thing."

He placed his hand over his forehead trying to prepare himself for what she was about to say. He felt the tears swell in his eyes and his heart begin to break.

"Michael, Michelle is in a coma and we don't know how long it will last. We just have to pray and be with her to help her come out of it. The doctor doesn't know if Michelle has suffered any brain damage because they are not able to run tests." She paused, trying to compose herself. "Michael are you still there?"

"Yes, I'm sorry." He sighed and got his strength to determine what needed to be done. "Look Nicole I'm going to get the first available flight to Pittsburgh tomorrow morning. I want to see Michelle. Could you do me a favor and meet me at the airport?"

"Sure, no problem. I'll give you my number. It's 412-555-2446. You call me the minute you get your travel arrangements and we'll take it from there. Michael when you get here I'll explain everything to you."

"Okay. Thanks a million Nicole. I'll see you tomorrow. And Michelle?"

"Yes?"

"Thank you for being there, otherwise I would have never known what was happening with Michelle."

She smiled and wiped the tears from her eyes. "Your very welcome Mr. Michael Morgan." She hung up and thought Michael to be more than just a friend to Michelle. Maybe Michelle just didn't see it at the time, but Nicole definitely could feel it from the phone conversation she just had with him.

She picked the receiver up again and dialed the number to Michelle's mother.

"Hello?"

None of the strange noises or odd voice was going to stop Nicole. After speaking with Michael the conversation had encouraged her in some odd way. "Hello, Mrs. Todds."

"Who is this?"

"Mrs. Todds...."

"This is Mrs. Garrett, who is this?" the tired voice asked again.

"I'm sorry Mrs. Garrett." Nicole looked back at the black book and wondered why Michelle never changed her mother's last name. "My name is Nicole Grant. I'm a friend of your daughter Michelle."

Barbara Jean Todds-Garrett sat up in her bed and glanced at her husband, careful not to disturb him. "What are you talking about?" she asked, whispering into the receiver. "I don't have a daughter!"

"Mrs. Todds, excuse me, Mrs. Garrett, with all due respect please hear me out. After I'm done if you don't want to acknowledge your daughter, fine. I'll never bother you again, but I think there is something you need to know about your daughter."

"Is this some kind of joke? I don't have a daughter."

"Oh but you do Mrs. Garrett, and soon your wish of denying your daughter may very well come true. Your daughter is in a coma." She announced the words before Mrs. Garrett would have the chance to hang up on her. She wanted her to hear the words and give her something to consider before slamming the phone down, which she knew was about to happen. "Mrs. Garrett are you still there?"

"Honey, who is on the phone?"

Nicole heard a deep voice and then Barbara Jean Todds-Garrett hung up.

She climbed under the sheets of her friend's bed and rock herself to sleep. The phone rang and she reached for it. "Hello?"

"Who is this?"

"This is Nicole. Who is this?"

"This is Robert Garrett, Michelle's father."

Nicole slowly rose up and leaned her back against the headboard of Michelle's bed.

"Did you call my wife last night?"

"Yes sir, I did."

"Well I'd like to talk to you, my wife has gone out. What was your reason for calling her? She seemed very upset this morning."

"Sir, I called to tell her, your daughter Michelle is in a coma."

Robert Garrett felt the sting of tears run down his cheek. They were tears for the thought of truly loosing her.

26
Friends

D onna, Stacie and Nicole sat at gate 47 in the airport. Michael's flight was not due to arrive until 8:35 AM. It was now 8:15 AM. All three women had taken the day off to meet Michael at the airport. Nicole had explained everything to Donna and Stacie. She told them about speaking briefly to Michelle's mother and how she had hung up on her. She also told how Mr. Garrett had called her the next morning.

She felt good that there was a chance they would be arriving at the airport sometime that day. No one was sure if it was a good idea for Mrs. Todds-Garrett to see her daughter or not. Both Donna and Stacie agreed it might have been the breaking point for Michelle to come out of the coma.

"I can't believe Michelle never told us about this Michael person," Stacie said. Nicole slapped her gently on the back. It felt good to have laughter again.

"Hey, anybody want anything? I'm going to walk down to the coffee shop," Donna announced getting up from her chair.

"Yeah, here." Stacie handed her a five-dollar bill. "Get me some decaffeinated tea."

"Now you know how hard it is to find that stuff here."

"Excuse me? I recall someone asking if anyone wanted anything. To me, that means anything, right? So get me what I want girl," Stacie told Donna smiling while hugging her.

"Okay," Donna said shaking her head. "I'll be right back."

Donna stopped in the gift shop before going to the coffee shop. She picked up a pretty porcelain tiger figurine. She gently placed it back in its proper place when she turned it over and saw the price tag. Then she growled at the tiger.

She finally made it to the coffee shop and told the young woman what she wanted. And they just so happened to have Stacie's decaffeinated tea. She pulled out her money and as she waited for her change she noticed a woman sitting in the corner alone. She rubbed her eyes because the woman looked just like Carmella. Maybe it wasn't, but she was going to find out.

"Carmella, is that you?"

When she looked at Donna she immediately knew it was Darletta. She could always tell them apart when she got close enough.

"Darletta, what are you doing here? Are you okay? You look terrible."

"It's none of your business why I'm here. And yes, I'm okay. Did I ask for your opinion on how I look?"

"Girl, I see you haven't changed. Where's Carmella?"

"I don't know, and I don't care!"

Donna could tell when she wasn't needed. She turned on her heals and went on about her business. Before returning to her sister and Stacie she stopped at the pay phone and dialed Carmella's number. With all that had been happening she hadn't spoken to Carmella in months. She felt she needed to know her sister was there.

"Hello?"

"Hi sweetie, it's me Donna. Listen I don't know if you know it or not, but your sister is here at the airport.

"Oh, so that's where she is." Carmella replied.

"Is everything all right Carmella? Your sister looks very strange. Is there something you want to talk about? You know I'm here if you need me. Where have you been anyway? I've been trying to contact you."

"I've been away on a last minute assignment for a flight to China." Carmella could feel her eyes fill with tears. She really needed a friend right now. And who better to confide in then her friend Donna. She knew talking to Donna would help her to see things more clearly.

"Carmella are you still there?"

"Yes, Donna, I'm sorry. So much has happened and I really do need to talk to you."

"Okay, when Carmella?"

"Today if it's at all possible. I could really use a lending ear." She began to cry as all the events that took place bellowed up inside of her. And she knew Donna would listen and give her sound advice.

"Carmella?" It broke her heart to hear the pain she was going through. And as sure as she was standing there, she knew it had something to do with her sister. "Carmella, I'm going to be leaving the airport shortly. As soon as I take care of this business I will come by to see you. I'm off today anyway. Will you wait there for me?"

"Yes, I'll be here Donna."

"Can I bring you anything?"

"No, I'm fine. I just need a friend right now."

"Well I'll see you in a bit."

"Okay. Thank you Donna. I love you," she told her as she wiped the tears running down her face.

"Ditto," she said, wishing she were there to hug her.

Carmella hung up wondering why Donna was at the airport and not at work. She felt bad, realizing that maybe Donna had her own dilemma she was dealing with and here she was crying about her own pain. She made a mental note to bring it up when Donna came over. She wanted to make sure she was okay before she bombarded her with the details of her distorted life.

Donna returned to where Nicole and Stacie were.

"Well it's about time. I know my tea is iced tea by now." Donna ignored Stacie's comment and told the women how she had just seen Darletta and had spoken to Carmella over the phone.

"There is definitely something wrong with Darletta and Carmella." Well their probably at their usual battle, you know how that Darletta is," Nicole said.

"I know that," Donna acknowledged. "But I think there is something very wrong with Carmella. I think something happened that has really hurt her this time. I'm going to go over to her house when were finished here."

"Okay, Stacie and I can get Michael to the hospital. We'll see you later, okay?" Nicole told her.

"Okay."

All three women looked to gate 47 as the attendant announced flight 428 had just arrived from California. Nicole could feel the anticipation that the others were feeling about finally meeting the mysterious man. The women moved over towards the entrance of gate 47. They watched tentatively as the passengers continued to greet their family and friends.

"Nicole, do we know what he's wearing?" Donna asked.

"Yes, he told me he would be wearing a short black leather jacket and jeans. I told him it was cold here."

"Well he sure does do something to old jeans and leather jackets. Girl, look at him!" Stacie nodded in the direction of the woman blocking everyone from getting to their family and friends.

"Girl he is fine! And didn't you say he was a doctor?" Stacie asked looking at Nicole.

"Mm!" she said nodding her head up and down. She kept her eyes on the bald brother.

Donna giggled softly because she could tell Michael was beginning to get frustrated. Finally the attendant came to his rescue and helped him out of the commotion. Michael stood looking relieved trying to find the women who agreed to meet him. He heard a familiar voice.

"Michael, hi over here." Nicole was waving her hand in the direction of which he was to follow.

Michael smiled, following her gesture. He held his hand out to Nicole and announced who he was. "Hi, I'm Michael Mason."

In But A Moment

Nicole smiled and returned the gesture. "Michael it's a pleasure to finally meet you. I'm Nicole." She was so busy staring at him she forgot to introduce him to Stacie and Donna.

"Isn't that Dr. Mason?" Stacie asked coming from around Nicole and reaching for Michael's hand.

He smiled. "Yes for my patients, but you can call me Michael." He placed his hand in Stacie and gave her a gentle squeeze. He found all three women to very attractive and pleasant.

Michelle had told him all about them. As he looked at them, he silently bet he could tell who was who. He couldn't remember the last time he was introduced to three beautiful women at the same time. The three women liked him immediately and wondered still why Michelle had never mentioned him to them before.

"Michael, we're going to go straight to the hospital, unless of course you want to change or something," Nicole stated.

"No, I'm fine. I really want to get to the hospital to see Michelle."

"Well, I'm going to drop my sister Donna off at a friend's house and she'll meet us back at the hospital." Then she remembered she never introduced Donna and Stacie. "Oh I'm sorry, Michael this is my sister Donna."

Donna extended her hand. "It's nice to meet you Michael."

"And this is our friend Stacie."

"Pleased to meet you Stacie."

"Like wise," she said. Stacie thought it didn't make any sense to be that fine and have a fine career to match. Michael stood 6'5" tall and weighed about 215 lbs. He had a dark shoe leather complexion. Small slanted eyes with very dark thick eyebrows, that almost bounced together when he smiled. He had the highest cheekbones she had ever seen on a man. Stacie thought something had to be wrong for Michelle to never mention him.

He smiled to himself and was glad he had met Michelle's friends. It touched him to see how much her friends loved and cared for her. He only wished he had met them on a different occasion.

27
A Phone Call Away

Eunice watched as Bill Tilmann walked towards his office. She really couldn't determine what type of mood he was in. She felt as though she was loosing her touch. She usually could pick up instantly what type of mood her boss was in. And that would determine the type of day she could expect.

Although he never treated her bad, she still liked to know how he was feeling. She shook her head and walked towards the coffee station to pour the sixth cup of coffee for the day.

Bill glanced at his watch. It was 8:45 AM. He decided to take the chance of calling Savassiea at home.

"Hello," said the pleasant voice on the other end.

"Hello back to you. This is Bill Til…."

"I know Bill, I recognize your voice," she told him feeling jocose.

"I thought maybe you would still be asleep," he said, knowing he was lying. He remembered her telling him she was an early bird.

"No, don't you remember I told you I'm always up with the birds. So what's up Mr. Tilmann?"

"I've just received the papers from our legal department. They are all signed sealed and ready for pickup or delivery, which ever you prefer. He was hoping she said pickup because he wanted to see her.

"Great, then everything is good to go?"

"Yep, sure is."

"Let's see." She tried to play with the thought of coming to visit with him, but then decided she may be to forward. She let him decide. "Bill, which ever you prefer is fine with me. Just let know."

"Okay I'll tell you what, let's have dinner tonight."

She could feel her heart pounding because she couldn't wait.

"How about that?" he asked.

"Great where and when?" She knew she had let her guard down now.

He knew from her voice despite her attempt of trying to hide her excitement she was pleased and looked forward already to the evening. "Okay, there's a cute little restaurant in Shady Side called the Room. Let's meet there at 7:00 PM. Do you know where it is?"

"Sure do, I'll see there then," she told him smiling all the while.

Eunice eased the receiver to its proper position. She knew that woman wanted more than a business deal with Bill. She knew it. Nothing could get pass her. But what could she want from Bill? She thought.

Bill placed one more call to Jackson's office.

"Jackson Waters."

"Hey man, it's me. How's it going?"

"Hey, it's the same."

"Did you take care of the business you needed to this morning?"

"Yes, I went first thing this morning to get the test. I should get the results back on Wednesday. Man I have never been so scared in all my life. Talk about praying, man I've been praying every second that I am negative."

"I can only imagine how you're feeling. Have you talked to Carmella?"

"No, I think I'll wait to see what the results are from my test before I talk to her."

"Is that cool though?"

"I'm just so angry right now I don't want to say something that I might regret later. So it's best I just chill with her."

"Has she tried to call you?"

"Yeah, I got six messages from her yesterday."

In But A Moment

"Well, man I'll say this. It's not Carmella's fault. I know she really wants to be there for you right now. Why don't you let her?"

Jackson rubbed his temples and sat back in his chair. He knew what his friend was saying was true. It really wasn't her fault that she didn't know what her sister was up to. That's why he was so adamant about not keeping secrets. Had she just introduced him to her sister or at least told him about her, maybe they wouldn't be in this mess. He knew in his heart that he still loved her.

"Hey, how's a what's her name again?"

"Savassiea," Bill said.

"Yes, how's she doing? Have you had an opportunity to speak to her?"

"As a matter of fact, we're going to have dinner tonight."

"Good man, I hope it works out. You're so smooth. I'm sure she won't be able to resist your charm," Jackson said, feeling a small gleam of hope for his friend. He wanted Bill to find the right woman and to be happy.

Bill laughed at his friend's comment. "Hey listen man. I've got to roll, but keep me posted on the results. And hey man, be encouraged."

"Hey, I will. Peace man."

Jackson hung up the phone and forgot all about the news he wanted to share with his friend. During his presentation, which went very well, he had the ability to meet a man by the name of Tate Robinson, who is an investment broker. He encouraged Jackson by informing him that he should take his talents elsewhere and he really should have his own business. He was willing to tell him how to do just that. Jackson was meeting with Tate later in the week. He was so rapped up in the situation he was going through that it completely slipped his mind. He made a mental note to call Bill later. He focused is mind back on the reports he was working on before Bill called him. And then he picked up the phone and called Carmella Springer.

28
<u>Welcome Back</u>

D onna tapped lightly on Carmella's door. She heard her
yell out she was coming. Carmella opened the door
and immediately hugged her friend. She was really
glad to see her. Donna returned her gesture and smiled as she
looked at Carmella.

Carmella looked as though she had been crying for a
very long time. Her usual teenage look somehow matured
rapidly. It looked as though her already small frame
diminished even further, which made her appear fragile.

Donna grabbed her friend's hand as Carmella lead her
to the kitchen. She walked over to the stove as Donna took a
seat at her kitchen table.

"I've just made a fresh pot of coffee, let me pour you a
cup," Carmella said speaking to her friend with her back
turned.

"Thanks I'd like that Carmella," Donna told her
smoothing out the place mat sitting in front of her. Donna
could sense her friend was very nervous about talking to her.
She wanted to find a way to make her feel comfortable.
Carmella turned and handed Donna the hot cup of coffee.
"Thanks," Donna said while staring into Carmella's eyes.

"Are you hungry Donna? I could fix us something,"
she said removing herself from the chair and walking towards
the refrigerator.

"Carmella come here," Donna told her patting her
hand on the opposite side of the table. "Please honey, sit
down. What's the matter Carmella? You know you can talk
to me, Girl. Now come on, tell me what's bothering you. Let
me help if I can."

Carmella began to cry. There was so much she wanted
to say but didn't know where to begin. How could she
possibly tell her friend, her sister may have exposed the AIDS

virus to her boyfriend? Maybe Donna wouldn't understand. But she knew in her heart that Donna would understand because she was just that type of person. The ringing of the phone allowed her a few more minutes of procrastination.

"Excuse me Donna I need to get that. Maybe it's my sister."

"Sure."

"Hello?"

"Hello, Carmella, it's me Jackson. I really need to talk to you. Do you have a few minutes? I'd like to come over."

"Jackson," she said beginning to feel more nervous. She played with the telephone cord wrapping it around her finger over and over again. Donna watched as she sipped her coffee. "Hmm, well, Donna is over here right now."

Donna looked up at Carmella, who was placing her finger over her lips to gesture silence from Donna.

"Well, if you think your friend will be there for a while I can come over later."

"No, it's fine. Come on over. I'd like you to meet my friend anyway."

"Okay, then I'll see you in about 30 minutes."

"Okay, see you then." She hoped whatever Jackson needed to speak to her about would allow them the ability to become an item again. She loved him so much. She hung up the phone and walked back over to where Donna was sitting.

"Was that Jackson, Carmella?" Donna asked in an inquisitive tone.

"Yes, he's coming over shortly. I'd really like you to finally meet him Donna. Will you stay?"

"Of course, I am going to stay, because you have yet to tell me what's going on with you."

Carmella looked down at the place mat in front of her and encircled the coffee cup with her index finger. "Okay." She took a deep breath and looked her friend in the eyes and prayed she'd help her to relieve herself of all the guilt she was feeling. "Okay, here it goes. Sit back Donna, and let me explain everything to you."

"I'm listening."

Donna was very quiet while Carmella spoke. She allowed her to say everything she needed to say without interruption. When Carmella finished Donna walked over to her friend and held her in her arms.

"Oh Carmella, I'm so sorry about everything that has happened." Life was so unfair at times. But, she refused to allow life's dilemmas to make her loose faith or dampen her spirit. And right now she was going to try her best to encourage her friend. She touched the side of her friend's face and wipes her tears away. "Baby none of this was your fault. Don't think that for a minute."

"But Donna, if I would have told Jackson everything from the beginning maybe this would not have ever happened."

"Carmella, you did that out of guilt from your sister. What happened to your sister was not your fault. You could not keep that kind of promise to her. But you felt as though you owed her something because you feel it should have been you. But honey, it wasn't you. The best thing you can do right now is try and get Darletta to get help. There are plenty of medications now available to treat HIV positive people. Also she needs to get into therapy. She has to learn to love herself again. It's going to be okay, you'll see, just be encouraged. Isn't Jackson on his way?"

"I don't think so Donna. Maybe he's coming by to give me the riot act. Maybe he blames me for all that has happened. He shouldn't have been involved." She began to cry again.

"Carmella, look at me!" Donna lifted her face towards her. "Jackson, loves you girl. And I doubt he is coming over here to lay you out. Did he sound upset when he called?"

"No, not at all."

"Well then, just wait and see what he has to say. Don't jump to conclusions."

Both women turned when they heard the knock on the door. Carmella rose from her seat and walked towards the door. Donna watched as she opened the door. Jackson stood outside for a minute while Carmella just stared at him.

"Well, can I come in?" he asked.

"Yes, I'm sorry Jackson." She moved back to allow room for him to enter. Carmella stood watching him with a solemn look on her face.

Jackson watched her and he knew there was no denying the fact that he loved her. And what had happened was not her fault. He thought about what Bill had told him. He needed Carmella and it was unfair to keep her out. He knew she still loved him. "Come here baby." She ran over to him and placed her head on his chest. "It's going to be okay, baby. It's going to be okay."

She smiled in his chest as the tears of joy escape her eyes. She was never so happy to have the two most important people in her life standing in her home allowing her to be herself and loving her. She only wished Darletta would forgive her and love her again. But, she thought about all the things Donna had just spoken to her about. She was going to get through to her sister and get her the help she needed. "Come here Jackson. I want you to meet my friend Donna Grant." She held his hand as she led him into the kitchen. "Donna, this is Jackson Waters."

Donna looked up from her second cup of coffee and smiled while extending her hand. "Pleased to meet you," she told Jackson. She continued to hold onto his hand. She felt like she had seen him before, but she just couldn't place her finger on where.

"Like wise," he said. The three of them sat down at the kitchen table and talked for hours. They all were in the need of uplifting.

Then Carmella remembered, "Donna, is everything okay with you? I forgot to ask you why you were at the airport."

"Yes, everything will be." Then she sat and told them what had happened to her friend Michelle and how they had just met a friend of hers at the airport who didn't know what had happened to Michelle.

She could tell the way they continuously looked at each other that they were happy to have things almost back to the way they use to be. She could tell by looking at Jackson that he loved her and was just as happy as Carmella to have her back in his life. Then it hit Donna, right when Jackson looked at Carmella. She remembered where she knew him from, the elevator several months before. That was him. He was the guy on the elevator she had seen. Donna sat looking at Jackson as if she had just seen a ghost.

"Donna, is something wrong?" Carmella asked.

"Oh, no," she laughed. "I just remembered where I've seen you before," she said looking at Jackson.

"Where?" Jackson asked looking mystified. Trying to flip back in his mind who he could have been in contact with. He knew he wasn't doing anything that he had to be ashamed of. But the look Donna gave him made him a little uneasy.

"On the elevator in the Fifth Avenue Place building several months ago. Remember? There was a white woman who had placed her hand in the elevator to stop it? I was so irritated by the way that woman peered at you and how you kept trying to acknowledge her. It was like you were breaking your neck to talk to this woman who was content with you not saying anything to her at all. And there I was, wishing you would at least act like I was a human being by at least saying hello. I was so angry with you, I remember trying to justify to myself why you wouldn't speak to me, yet hold a conversation with a white woman you didn't even know. You know how sisters are about white woman and y'all make it worse when you can't even have the decency to speak to us. You know that's a reason for a roll of the eyes and a swing of the head!" she said smiling as she watched for his reaction. "It made me think that you didn't like the sisters."

"Okay," he said smiling at her. "I remember that day. I viewed it a little differently though. I was about to say hello to you, and you looked at me like don't even try it cause I ain't in the mood! I thought oh she's one of those stuck up type of women. So I figured it's best for me to just stare straight at the elevator buttons." They both laughed.

"See if we would've of just said hello to each other we wouldn't have assumed about the other."

"You're right," he told her. "We do have that tendency to think a certain way before we part our lips to speak to each other. Well, I will apologize if you thought I was being a real jerk."

"The reason why I spoke and acted the way I did with that white woman you saw on the elevator was because she works with me and I know for a fact she can't stand me, because of my position. Therefore, I do what I can to irritate her to no end. I make a point to make her speak when she sees me, cause I know she hates it. But, you're right we shouldn't assume negative about each other. So am I forgiven?"

"Sure, I'm glad we had an opportunity to meet to clear up the differences we had."

She smiled and winked at Carmella. Carmella returned the wink and mouthed the words I love you to her.

"Ditto," she mouthed back.

"Well, I guess I better get going. I need to get to the hospital." She pulled her coat from the back of the chair and placed it over her shoulders.

"Thank you Donna for everything," Carmella said while reaching to hug her.

"Stay sweet, and remember what I said about your sister. Let me know what you want me to do and in the meantime. I'll be working on something on my end. Okay?"

"Okay."

Jackson walked towards her to hug and thank her.

"Why are you thanking me Jackson?"

"For helping my baby and for giving a brother some slack."

"You're so crazy!" she said, returning the hug. "I'll see you later." She smiled and waved as she walked out the door.

Carmella shut the door behind Donna and walked back to the kitchen. Jackson followed and they sat and talked for hours. She let him know that no matter what the out come was she would always be there for him. And she meant just that. She curled up on the couch next to him and was happy to be in his arms again. "Thank you God," she whispered.

29
<u>The Single Truth</u>

Bill stepped into the steaming water and held his face to it's tingling bristle. He sang softly under the water's pulsating beat. His spirits were grand and he felt as though he owned the whole world. The love bug had finally bitten him and he wasn't one bit sore from its teeth. He just wanted to be able to tell Savassiea how he felt.

He never thought it would ever get a hold of him. He was so content with just being able to date different women and come home to the quietness of his house. But, he now realized the quiet house was truly not a home without someone to share it with. He felt he had now found that someone and he was willing and able to announce to this woman what he was feeling.

He stepped out of the shower and dried off. Then he walked to the kitchen and poured himself a tall glass of spirits. As he continued back to the bathroom to shave the ringing of the phone forced him to detour to the living room.

"Yeah, hello."

"Bill," he heard a crying voice on the other end announce.

"Yeah, Mom is that you? What's wrong?" He felt his heart sink. The cry of his mother paralyzed him. He tried to calm Victoria Tilmann down, but to no avail. "Mom, please calm down I can't understand what you are saying." He was very afraid now. He thought something had happened to his father. And though he despised the man, he was still his father. And if something happened to him he knew how devastated his mother would be. He tried again to find out what had happened. "Mom did something happen to Dad?"

Hearing her son say dad helped her to gain her composure again. It was confirmation that her son still cared about his father and that told her there was still hope. "I'm sorry honey. It's not your dad. It's Ayreonna." Then she began to get hysterical again.

"Ayreonna? Mom what happened to Ayreonna?" He heard himself yelling at his mother. He needed to know what was going on. Through her crying and whimpering she managed to tell him that his father's daughter had been hit by a car and was now in the Hospital about to be operated on.

"Baby, she has lost so much blood, their talking about her needing a blood transfusion. Your Dad has already offered to supply his blood to her." She held her head against the wall in the hospital lounge as her husband sat with his head in his hands crying. "It doesn't look good son, if they can't give her back the amount of blood she lost she may die."

"Mom, look I'm going to catch the next flight out of Pittsburgh. I should be there shortly. I'll come straight to the hospital. And, Mom, don't worry she's a strong little girl she'll make it."

"I hope so honey. I've asked the good Lord to cover her with his blood. We just have to pray son."

"Okay Mom." He didn't have time for her lectures on prayer. He needed to get to his little sister. He didn't know what he would do if that little girl died. He loved her so much. He clicked the phone off and realized he needed to call Savassiea to let her know he wasn't going to be able to make dinner. He dialed her number. "Please be home Savassiea."

She answered on the fourth ring. "Hello?"

"Hey Savassiea, it's me Bill." She could immediately tell something was not right with his tone.

"Bill, what's up? Is something wrong?"

"Yes, a family emergency has come up I need to fly to Washington right now. I'm calling because we are going to have to postpone our dinner engagement."

Her heart began to pound. What type of family emergency was he talking about? "Bill what happened?"

"I don't have time to get into it with you right now. My sister and my mom really need me."

"Bill, listen to me. I will go with you. You don't need to travel alone." She knew now she had to tell him the truth before Bill had the opportunity to find out when he got to the hospital. She had to tell him now.

"That's really sweet of you, but I don't won't to inconvenience you. After all, it is my family and you've never met them. It may be rather awkward."

"No, really it's not an inconvenience. I want to be with you to help you through this. Please let me come along." She waited for his response. Then she felt the twitch on the side of her mouth start.

It touched him that she was so concerned and it also confirmed what he had known. She was in love with him. He really could use her company. "Okay, Savassiea, can you get here in the next 15 minutes?"

"Yes, I'm leaving right now." She hung up and whispered thank you. "Please, please give me the words to say to him and the courage to do this before we arrive at the hospital. Oh and please, please let that little girl makes it."

Bill hung up and made the necessary arrangements for a flight to Washington, DC.

It seemed like hours before Bill and Savassiea were finally seated on the plane and heading towards Washington. She listens as Bill talked about Ayreonna and how he loved her. He told her how he always had this bond with her and could never figure out why. He disclosed to her the deception Doris and his father had bestowed upon him. He even cried at one point talking about the whole ordeal. She reached up to him and wiped his tears and told her it was going to be okay.

"Bill there's something I need to tell you, that's very important. But before I do, I need to tell you something else first."

He watched her wondering where she was going with the conversation. Though he was upset and had mixed emotions as far as his sister and father, he was not prepared for what she was about to disclose to him.

158

In But A Moment

Savassiea held his hand in hers and looked him in his eyes. She could feel the love she felt deep within her. She wanted to spend the rest of her life with him and love him the way he deserved to be loved. She knew in her heart he loved her and the anticipation was driving her crazy. She wanted to get up at that very moment and shout out to everyone seated on the plan that she loved him. But, she knew after she disclosed the information regarding Ayreonna his feelings may change towards her. And she knew in but a moment everything was going to change.

She continued to stare into his beautiful green eyes. Bill returned her stare. "Savassiea, what is it?"

"Bill, I love you." She had said it with closed eyes and was afraid to open them. Slowly she lifted her eyes to him. "I love you Bill," she said again. "I've loved you from the moment I first saw you. I knew then that you were the one for me.

He placed his fingers over her lips and all the emotions he had bubbling inside came to surface. "Savassiea, I feel the same way. I love you too. And I knew you were the one for me. I want to spend the rest of my life with you. No other woman has ever touched me the way that you have. You mean everything to me and my mission will be to make you the happiest woman in the world if you give me the opportunity to prove my love to you." He wiped away the tears she was now spilling and continued to speak to her in a monotone voice. She reached over and kissed him tenderly on the lips and hugged him. He didn't know how happy he had just made her. Only she was afraid now, for there was more to what she had to say. It would determine if the love he just expressed to her would be solid. She closed her eyes and prayed for the right words to tell him he was going to be by his daughter's side not his stepsister. She didn't want to hurt him but she knew he had to know.

She didn't want to keep any secrets from him she wanted to love him wholeheartedly. And in order to achieve that, she had to be honest with him. Everything needed to be told. She watched him as he leaned his head back against the seat still holding her hand. He closed his eyes, and at moments she saw a smile on his face.

"Bill?"

"Yeah?"

"There's something else I need to tell you." He sat up and looked at her.

"What?"

"Bill I need to know, when I tell you this you will still love me and believe in me."

He looked distressed. "Well, yes. What is it?" He thought that maybe it was too good to be true. Maybe she had some type of disease that would cause him to loose her. He wasn't prepared for any more drama.

All the emotions he was feeling now made him feel excited yet distraught. He wanted her to say what it was she had to say so he could feel whatever emotions he needed to feel complete. He was tired and beginning to feel down.

Savassiea rubbed the back of his hand. "Bill I don't know how to say this."

"Savassiea just say it, come on now, you're making me very nervous!"

"Bill, I knew Doris Richardson very well. In fact she was my best friend."

He slowly removed his hand from her and looked her deep in her eyes. "What was going on here? Was this some type of joke?" He could feel past emotions of Doris flow back to his heart. And it was breaking his heart in two.

Savassiea leaned forward positioning her body to face him. "Bill I loved Doris very much and I would not be doing what I'm about to do unless I did love her. I've given it a great deal thought and consideration. Bill before Doris died she had made out a Will. It was something she and I did a long time ago as friends, never thinking we would need to use it so soon. Doris had a request for me before she died. She had cancer. The doctors told her she needed to begin chemotherapy as soon as possible. Although she was pregnant, they told her she needed to make a choice. If she didn't begin chemotherapy as soon as possible, she would die. And if she began the chemotherapy she would survive, but the medication would be to severe for the baby to survive." She looked at Bill hoping she would get some type of response. But she didn't, he just sat there staring into space and feeling numb.

"She never told anyone Bill, not even your father. She made me promise not to say anything. She had already determined she was not going to take the chemo, because she wanted to spare the life of her child. She wanted to revise her Will. And in it she stated that no one was to know what she included in her Will other than me. Bill, she never told me what she had written in the Will and I was contacted after her death and it was read to me from a letter."

She searched through her purse until she found it and handed it to him. He took the letter and read what Doris had written. On the outside in big bold letters it stated, "Do Not Read Until The Time of My Death".

Bill opened the letter and read with much concentration.

Dear Save,

I write you this letter allowing you the time to mourn over my death, however I don't want you to mourn to long (smiles). I love you very much and you mean the world to me. Through all my decisions I've made throughout life you have always been very supportive of me (even when you did not totally agree) and I just want to let you know that I've really appreciated it and I thank you.

You have been a true friend to me and I know that God had a lot to do with us becoming such good friends for he

Shérri A. Gambrill

never let us part in our friendship. I am truly grateful. I can name four great blessings he has bestowed upon me. (1) The presence of his spirit, which is now in me, (2) a molded friend he gave especially to me (3) a man of great vitality (4) and the child growing inside me.

The decision I've made to allow my life to end for the sake of my baby is not a decision I've made in vain. For I know he/she will be taken care of. I know she or he will be beautiful and grow to be a prominent man or women. Especially if she mines her father and inherits his strong sense of character and ambitious nature.

You know I've never stopped loving that man. I was such a fool to allow myself to get into something so deep. I guess I just never had patience - how patience is truly a virtual! I know that he is a well-rounded man and he has accomplished so many things in life and will continue to do so. His daughter or son will have a great Dad, someone they will be proud of. But, my friend, there's something I need you to do once my child is born. I don't know how long it will be before you have the courage to do this. Cause I know you, never wanting to be placed in the middle. But, I also know you would do anything in the world for me.

My friend, please disclose to the man I have never stopped loving, Bill Tilmann that the son or daughter I give birth to is his daughter or son. I'm sorry I never had the courage to tell him. I hope it's a girl. He always wanted a daughter, to name her Ayreonna Ann. I've already told William that's what I wanted to name my child if it is a girl.

I've never stopped loving Bill, but I was just into something to deep to get out of. I never wanted to hurt him, truly I didn't. If I could turn the hands of time back I would do things so differently. But I know everyone makes mistakes.

162

In But A Moment

Mine was to go off with his father, but I am glad Bill and I were able to conceive this child, this Angel.

I know I was selfish and young and didn't understand the beauty of true love. Bill is a good man and he is going to make some woman very, very happy. I've asked God to forgive me for the wrongs I have done and I know that he has done that, and I am at peace. I will always watch over my little girl (God revealed to me it's a girl - smile - your godchild) and knowing that Bill knows the truth about her, I will be at a quiet peace and able to enjoy the joyful noise of Heaven.

I love you!
Be at Peace and shed no more tears for me, I'm okay with God!

D!

Bill crumbled the letter up in his hand and cried so hard that the stewardess came over to ask if everything was okay. Savassiea told her yes and then held Bill as he allowed his emotions to take over. He knew he had to get to his daughter.

He lifted his head and looked at Savassiea. "My daughter? O God. Please God, don't let her die. Hold on baby girl, please hold on." He allowed the essence of grief to absorb his spirit. He never knew Doris had loved him still and to think she gave him the most precious gift he could ever had asked for. And now his baby was fighting for her life.

"Bill," Savassiea called softly. "Baby, are you okay?"

"No, but I will be I've got to get to my baby and let her know that her daddy's here. Savassiea wondered if he was going to let her go, now that she had disclose the necessary information. Maybe he needed time to gather all she had said.

She'd wait if she needed to. And just as if he read her mind, he placed her hand back in his and smiled.

"I'm about to have the two most important women in my life for good."

"I love you," she told him and removed the crumbled letter from his hand.

30
My Child

Barbara Jean Todds-Garrett sat in the front seat of their truck. She was so afraid to continue into the hospital to see her child fighting for her life. It took her husband hours before he could convince his wife that their daughter needed them. He always considered Michelle as his own daughter.

She needed them now and he was determined to get his wife to attend to their daughter. He was not a man who held grudges, nor was he a man who was going to sit back while his daughter stayed in a hospital without her family by her side to encourage her, to pray for her and to love her the way she so desperately needed.

All the ill feelings from the past fled immediately to the surface for Barbara. She knew deep down she never was the mother Michelle so desperately needed. She was a victim of rape when she got pregnant with Michelle. She didn't believe in abortion. So she had Michelle and carried the guilt of being raped with her.

She felt so dirty when it had happened and she cried for hours. Every time she'd looked into Michelle's eyes she despised her. But, she thought she could learn to love her the way a mother should love a daughter. She knew deep down it wasn't Michelle's fault. But she didn't know how to love someone she felt was a product of filth, she never told her only daughter her father was white and a rapist. She could never bring herself to tell her.

So instead she treated her like she was not her daughter. She wanted Michelle to go start a new life without her. Her husband was the only living soul she had told. Her husband tried to encourage her and tell her she needed to show love to her daughter. She wanted that more than anything but she just didn't know how to do it because she was so filled

165

with guilt. But today, as she sat in the truck she was afraid that she would loose her only daughter. She could never have any other children after Michelle. Yet she wanted her out of her life. Every time she would look at Michelle she'd see that night when she was raped.

All the times she wanted her daughter to move on. She wanted her to live now. After her talk with her husband, she realized that she really loved her daughter and if God would just spare her life she make it all up to her. To face the realization of actually seeing her daughter dead would be too much for her. She just wanted a second chance with her if she would allow it. She sat thinking about all the awful things she said to her little girl. Michelle was an innocent child wanting her mother's love.

Robert walked to the passenger side of the truck to help his wife out. Barbara cried softly while watching this wonderful man, who had been though so much pain and hurt, as he tried to console her and support her anyway he could.

He was saddened that it had to take a tragedy to make his wife realize how important and blessed she really was with Michelle. Now this child was fighting and fighting hard to survive. And there may be a chance he or his wife may never see her again and it frightened him. He opened the door for his wife and slowly, Barbara removed herself from the seat. He helped her into the hospital.

"Hello, my I help you sir?" the friendly woman said sitting at the reception desk.

"Yes, I'm Mr. Robert Garrett and this is my wife Barbara Jean Garrett, our daughter was brought here and we'd like to see her.

"What's the patient's name please?"

"Michelle Todds?"

The woman looked up from her computer and viewed the two individuals in an inconspicuous way. She didn't want to allow them the opportunity to know what she was thinking.

In But A Moment

She wondered how could they just now be coming to see their daughter?

"I'm sorry sir, but you are going to have to speak with your daughter's doctor. Neither of your names is on the visiting list for Michelle. I'm sorry. I'll page Dr. Bradshore right now and he can tell you about your daughter."

Dr. Bradshore explained Michelle's conditions to the Garretts. He was taking them to the CCU of the hospital for them to see their daughter. He was pleased that someone was able to finally locate them. Maybe their visit would help Michelle come out of the coma. It was worth a try. Once exiting the elevator, Dr. Bradshore instructed them to have a seat in the lounge area. Meanwhile he would see if it was a good time to see their daughter. He knew Michelle's friends were visiting with her. Dr. Bradshore entered the CCU and saw Stacie, Nicole and Donna standing outside the window of Michelle's room. The ladies smiled when they saw him approach.

"Why are you guys standing out here?"

"Oh because we wanted to give Michael, Michelle's friend sometime alone with Michelle," Stacie announced.

Dr. Bradshore looked through the window and saw a handsome man holding Michelle's hand and stroking her face.

The doctor turned around and announced to the women that Michelle's parents were there. They all looked surprise, although they knew there was a chance they would show up.

"I'm going to allow them some time with their daughter. How long has Michelle's friend been in there?"

"A little over 30 minutes," Donna said.

"Okay, well I'm going to allow her parents to come in for a few minutes. Could someone let Michael know that?"

"Yes. I will," Nicole announced.

In a few moments Michelle's friends were all standing outside her room waiting for the arrival of her parents. Donna could feel the tears running down her face as she watched Mr.

Garrett hold his wife up while helping her to the area. She was a very attractive woman. And she and her husband made a handsome couple. Nicole walked towards them and introduced herself and the others.

Barbara Jean smiled and continued into the room. "Thank you for calling us Nicole," she whispered.

When she finally got into Michelle's room she began to cry long exhaling gulps. She was so torn and felt so guilty with what had happened to her daughter. Mr. Garrett walked over towards Michelle and kissed her gently on her hand. He told his wife he would leave her alone and that she needed to tell Michelle everything she had told him last night. She shook her head in agreement.

She picked her daughter's limp hand up and held it to her face as she cried softly. "Michelle, my darling it's me Mom. I love you baby. I'm so sorry honey for everything I've caused to happen in your life. I know I wasn't a very good mother. I know I wasn't there for you. I also know that I've said some horrible things to you. I only hope you can and will forgive me. Even though I was going through my own bitterness, I had no right to take it out on you. Of course I would understand if you never forgave me Michelle. I had no right to treat you the way I did."

She tried to find her daughter's eyes and it broke her heart that she was not able to. Michelle's face was covered as well as her head. She wanted to have another chance with her, if only she could start all over again. She looked outside of Michelle's window and smiled at the friends Michelle had made. They loved her and that made her feel good.

She wondered now if she could ever recapture the time lost between them. She was so helpless now. So many times she wanted Michelle to feel helpless and exclude her from her life. Now here she was praying she would allow her to be a part of her life for good.

"Oh my God, what have I done to my own daughter?" She squeezed Michelle's hand.

In But A Moment

Robert slowly walked in as he watched his wife trying to rekindle something with her only child. It broke his heart to see them both in the condition they were in. He felt so helpless. He wanted to put everything back to the way it should have been so long ago. He walked over to where his wife was sitting and he pulled the small chair from against the wall over to Michelle's bedside. He reached over for his wife's hand as he held his daughter's hand. Robert Garrett looked at his wife flabbergasted, for he just felt Michelle gently squeeze his hand.

"What?" his wife asked.

"Oh my God!" he said in a very meek voice.

"What? What?" his wife continued to ask.

"She just squeezed my hand! She can hear us baby, she can hear us! Isn't it beautiful?" He cried liked a baby in the bosom of his daughter. Barbara ran out the room and called for the doctor. Dr. Bradshore ran into Michelle's room. He checked her vitals and held Michelle's hand.

"Michelle if you can hear me squeeze my hand one time." She squeezed and the doctor looked at her parents. He then removed the covering from over her eyes. She slowly opened her eyes and tried to focus in on her surroundings. She looked over at her mother and father. She moved her fingers towards her mother. Barbara held her daughter's hand and cried openly.

"Michelle did you hear all that I said to you honey?"

"Yes," she whispered. "I forgive you Mom and I love you." Then she looked over towards her father. "Daddy, I'm sorry for the lie I told. I truly love you. Please tell my friends I love them and thank them for me."

A small smile came upon her face as the tears rolled out the side of her eyes. She was happy and she knew she had to have her mother, father and her friends there when she said good-bye. She knew she'd meet them all again one day in a much greater place then where they were now. She had prayed a silent pray that God would just grant her the time to say good-bye to her parents. And he did. She knew she would be with him for he was in her spirit. And as her tears stopped and her smile remained, the machines stopped.

Barbara looked at her husband and screamed. "No! No! God No!"

Dr. Bradshore helped the couple to their feet and led them out the room. Barbara had become so hysterical that Michelle's friends came running out of the lounge area.

"What?" Nicole yelled. "What's wrong? What happened?"

Donna and Stacie stood watching from a distance, for they knew their friend was gone. They hugged each other as the tears sprang freely from their eyes.

"I'll see you in heaven," Donna whispered while looking at Michelle's room.

Stacie walked over to the Garretts and hugged them as Mrs. Garrett cried with her daughter's friend. They all walked out together. Michael stayed and held Michelle in his arms and cried as he rocked her.

"What I'm I going to do without you my friend? What I'm I going to do without you?" He gently laid her back down on the bed and took a final look at her. He smiled for he knew she had heard him when he told her he loved her and wanted to marry her.

Everyone was trying to console each other. For they knew Michelle would have wanted them all to finally meet and be friends. They also knew she wanted her mother to love her again. And she did.

31
<u>And Life Goes On</u>

J ackson sat nervously while watching the television
show. He felt talk shows were so stupid. It was as
though they thrived on seeing people get hurt or hurting
someone. He didn't even know why he was watching it. It
was the day he would get his test results back so he used a
vacation day. There was no way he could go into work not
knowing whether he was a walking time bomb. And if he
was, he'd rather be at home receiving the news than at his
office.

He grabbed the phone before the first ring was
completed. "Hello," he said sounding more anxious than
pleasant.

"Hey baby, any news yet?"

"No, in fact I thought you were the clinic."

"No, I was hoping you hadn't heard anything yet. I'm
coming over to keep you company until they call. Okay?"

"Okay, come on over." He could use the company
since he was so nervous.

He was trying to prepare himself if the results would
come back positive. He really didn't know as much as he
thought about the disease until he began to read up on it. He
sat and thought about all the things left to accomplish in his
life. And how proud he was for the things he had already
accomplished. He wondered if Carmella would really
continue to have a relationship with him if his test did come
back positive. He wondered about Bill, would he still be as
close to him as he is now? He wanted to prepare himself for
the worse.

He began reading every article he could get his hands
on to learn about being HIV positive and the AIDS virus. He
never really gave it much thought until now. How stupid he
was to not be protected. This whole ordeal had changed his

life tremendously. It proved to him that the disease will affect anyone.

The light tapping at the door startled his thoughts. Carmella walked in and hugged him. He stood there staring at her and wondering how she really would feel if she found out that he did in fact have AIDS. Would she remain there for him? Or would she carry on with her life? Deep down he knew what the answers were. She would be there for him.

"Hey, you had lunch yet?" she asked removing her coat.

"Nah, I'm not hungry."

"Okay, well do you mind if I fix myself a sandwich?"

"Go right ahead." He wanted to hold and kiss her and make love to her, but he was too afraid. He promised himself that he would not make love with her until he knew where he stood as for as being HIV positive or not. He went back to the living room. As he continued his walk the phone rang.

Carmella immediately stopped what she was doing and held her breath.

"Hello," Jackson said.

"Hello, Mr. Waters?"

"Yes!"

"This is Central Medical Center calling, we have the results of your test."

"Yes," he responded. He could feel his heart pounding. His hands began to perspire as tiny beads formed along his forehead.

"Can you hold on a minute while I transfer you to a counselor?"

"Yes," he said. Now he was really nervous. He thought the only reason they transfer you to a counselor is because it's bad news, otherwise she could have just told him the test came back negative. Why would he need to speak to a counselor if the test was negative?

"Hello, Mr. Waters, my name is Martha Goodwich. I'm the counselor they have assigned you to."

In But A Moment

"Okay, well are you going to tell me my results?" He could care less about who she was. He just wanted to know his fate. All this stalling was beginning to cause him serious pain. He just wanted this woman to announce the words positive or negative. Why did they have to go through all of this?

Carmella still stood in the kitchen to paralyzed to move. She'd just wait until Jackson was off of the phone to tell her the status of his results. If only she had been honest with him in the beginning about everything that had happened between her, Jerome and her sister this would never had escalated.

Jackson held his breath. "Mr. Waters, your test came back negative." He stood there for a moment, closed his eyes and breathed again. "I must insist Mr. Waters that you be tested in six months to be sure your are definitely not infected."

"I thought you said my test came back negative!" He began to get worried again.

"Yes, that's correct. However in order to be sure, you should be tested again. Sometimes it may take time for the virus to show up. This way, you can be sure you're not infected. In the meantime, I encourage you to use precautionary measures when engaging in sexual activities."

"So your telling me that there could be a chance I really am infected, it just hasn't shown up yet?"

"Mr. Waters, I really don't think you need to worry. The second test is just a precautionary measure we use so we are absolutely sure and you are. Statistics have shown that when a person is tested the first time usually 9 times out of 10 the next test will come out with the same result. So don't worry, just be careful when engaging in sex. As I have told all my patients, the best antidote is abstinence or if you are married, you and your wife should be tested to be sure neither of you are carrying the disease and then live a honest monogamist life together. Good luck Mr. Waters and I will

173

see you in six months." She spoke it more like a question than a statement.

Jackson smiled. "Yes, I'll see you in six months. Thanks." He hung up and shouted for Carmella. She ran into the living room knowing by the sound of his excitement he was not infected. He explained everything that the counselor had told him. He felt in his heart that he was going to be fine. Carmella reached up and kissed him tenderly on the lips. She loved him and she knew he was going to be okay. Life was good and pleasant and everything was in perfect order again.

He felt like celebrating. He held her face in his hands. "Hey baby, let's get dressed up and go out to a really nice restaurant and have a grand meal."

"Fine by me,"she said.

"And then let's go dancing. Remember that red dress I brought you when we first started dating?"

"Uh huh!" she told him looking puzzled.

"Well hey, wear that again."

"Where are we going to go for dinner?" she asked.

"I feel like splurging! Let's go to Morton's."

She smiled up at him. "You must really feel like splurging honey." If that was what he wanted she was all game.

"Okay then, I'm going to make reservations for 7:00 this evening, and you're going to wear that red dress right? Oh and wear it the way I like it!"

"And just how is that?" she teased.

"You know, bare. Oh with those high heeled red pumps too."

"Gee is there anything else you want Mr. Waters?" she whispered.

"Yes, wear you're hair pulled high on your head with those long earrings I like to see you in."

She smiled and kissed him on the cheek. "Okay, my darling if it will make your celebration complete. I'm going to go and have my nails done, so I'll wait for you to come pick me up, what around 6:15 PM?"

"Yes, I'll see you then Spicy." She smiled and headed towards the door.

"Oh baby," he yelled out at her. "I have one more thing I want you to wear." He went upstairs to his bedroom.

"Ah come on baby, I don't think there's anything left."

He walked over to her. "Will you wear this for me?" he asked pulling from behind his back, a small black velvet box.

"Jackson what is this?"

"Open it," he said.

She obliged, and a 2-carat diamond ring surrounded with baguettes sparkled at her.

"Oh my God! Jackson, Baby, Baby, what is this? It's so beautiful. I've never seen a more beautiful ring in my life," she whispered.

He removed the box from her hand, removed the ring from the box and held her hand. "Carmella Springer will you marry me? I love you with all my heart. I will take care of you all of my days. I will honor you, respect you and cherish you like the queen you are to me. I will caress your heart with the warmth of my love that will never change. I will secure your future with the works of my labor. I will love you all my days." He wiped away the tears from her eyes and hugged her. "Does that mean yes?" he asked.

"Yes!" she said, stroking his face. I love you so much and I will love you for the rest of my days.

He held her in his arms and smiled. "Now, go get ready we have lots of celebrating to do!"

She sat in her car continuing to stare at the beautiful piece of jewelry. She slipped it off her finger and examined it. She noticed there was a small inscription inside that read "I will love you all of my days JAW." She smiled and cried and thought who said a good man is hard to find?

32
<u>God works in Mysterious ways</u>

I t was music to everyone's ears when the doctor told them Ayreonna was going to be just fine. She would only have to stay in the hospital for a couple more days and then she would be free to go home. It turned out the transfusion was not needed after all. "That's God healing her body," Victoria announced. She knew how powerful the power of pray was and she trusted it everyday.

When Bill introduced her to Savassiea she liked her immediately and she knew she loved her son. If loving her was going to allow Bill peace of mind and the ability to show a little forgiveness towards his father, she was happy.

Bill broke the news about Ayreonna to both his mother and father. At first his father thought he was lying. Savassiea showed him the letter Doris had written. Tears welled up in his father's eyes and for the first time Bill knew his father was facing the same pain he had once felt towards the same woman. Only this time it was Bill who was getting the blessing. Although William was losing a daughter he was also gaining a granddaughter.

Victoria was happy either way; she had already forgiven her husband for his adulterous behavior. She had been praying day in and out that her husband and son would regain the love they had once shared for each other. And she knew again, God was working his miracle. When Bill saw the hurt in his father's eyes he reached out to him and held him and his father held on even tighter to his son. William Tilmann loved his son and he had been a fool to destroy his relationship with his son over a woman.

He could not have asked for a better woman than he had at that very moment. Victoria Tilmann was a God-fearing woman, which allowed her to forgive when forgiveness was warranted, however, she was not a stupid woman. The spiritual side of her being allowed her to witness the comfort of knowing all was not lost. It allowed her the comfort of knowing she had someone to talk to, to cry to and most of all vent her frustration out on. For she knew God was a gentleman and he loved her no matter what her state of mind was.

Many nights she cried knowing her own husband ran off with her only son's girlfriend. What could be worse than a father betraying his own flesh and blood? She despised William for a long time, but she never gave up on prayer and the hope that her family would one day coming back together. She saw now what God was trying to show her. It was not to loose faith and trust, but to believe that he will direct your path. So she stopped trying to find a method of revenge. She let Go and let God. And God did just what he said. He made it all right again. He brought her family back together and cleansed her husband with a sweet spirit. She knew he was real to her and no one could ever change her feelings toward her Lord and Savor. She could do nothing but praise him.

William was thankful he had a God-fearing woman and that she continued to remain his wife. Since the incident with Ayreonna he had tried listening to a lot of what his wife had been saying about God. He began going to church and bible studies with her. And he believed there was a higher power. How could that had happened without the help of some higher power. He realized he was truly blessed as he continued to cry in his son's chest.

Savassiea watched from a distance as she felt the tears roll down her face, it was a beautiful reunion for her to witness and somehow be a part of. She glanced at Bill's mother and saw her with her hands extended towards the heavens continuously praising God. She began to speak in some foreign tongue crying and smiling the whole time. Then and only then did she join her husband and son?

It was a savored moment for Savassiea to witness and she would never forget it. She was glad she had something to do with bringing Bill and his family back together.

Victoria glanced up at the young woman watching their reunion. She held her arm out for Savassiea to come and join them. She did just that, she moved closer to Victoria and held on to her hand. She kissed him tenderly on the lips and smiled. She was very grateful to be accepted into their family with open arms.

The doctor stood in the middle of the waiting area. "Excuse me, but I have a very eager little girl wanting to see her family. Anyone interested?" he asked smiling at the fact that the little girl was going to be okay.

Bill wondered how he was going to explain to his once half-sister that he was now her father. It was a task he knew would be a little awkward at first, however, he was determine to let his little girl know he was her daddy. Savassiea had agreed to assist in any way he may need her.

He briefly discussed with his parents their desire to get married. He suggested they get married in their home with their family's minister marrying them. They agreed. Bill told his parents he wanted something small and intimate with just the two of them, their daughter and parents and of course he was going to asked Jackson and Carmella. He and Savessiea wanted to get married soon. As soon as next week he announced. He and Savassiea would discuss later where they were going to live. Now that he had his daughter with them, he would need a bigger place. He was thinking about moving back home, transferring his business. He wanted his daughter to have close contact with her grandparents.

Then he remembered about Jackson receiving his news today about the test. He told his family to go ahead in and see Ayreonna and he'd be there shortly. He spotted a pay phone down the hall and dialed Jackson's number. After three rings Jackson picked up.

"Hello?"

"Hey man, it's me."

"Where are you? You sound like you're far away."

"I'm in DC. It's a long story, I'll explain it to you when I get back home. I was calling to find out about the test thing, how did it go?"

"Great! My test came back negative. Although I do have to go back in six months to be re-tested."

He could feel his friend smiling on the other end. "Ah man, that's great news! I'll bet that's a relief, huh?"

"You bet. I'm about to pick my fiancé up for a celebration dinner in a short while." He waited for his friend's response to his comment.

"Fiancé? What? Are you telling me you and Carmella got engaged? What happened? I can't believe it. That's really great man. I'm really happy for you. I'm glad you were able to work it all out. I really am." He smiled the whole time he was talking to his friend. "Are you sure were not related somewhere down the line?"

"Why do you say that?" Jackson asked.

"Because I have something to tell you too."

"What? Ah don't tell me you and Savas…."

"Yep, you got it! I've asked her to marry me. And she said yes. It's so wild how this all happened. I really want to explain everything to you. You're really not going to believe it."

"My boy, I can't believe someone finally got you to settle down, after all this time. I'll be!" He smiled. "Seriously man, I'm happy for you too. I know she has got to be pretty special for you to want to spend the rest of your life with her."

"That she is!" He smiled just thinking of her.

"We've decided to get married next week at a private ceremony at my parent's home. I'd love for you to be my best man and for Carmella to stand for Savassiea. She really doesn't have friends here. Oh and one more thing, I have a daughter!"

Jackson could hear the happiness in his voice and he was happy for his friend. "A Daughter? Y'all sure do work fast!" he said laughing.

"Hey, I'll explain it all to you when I get back in town. You'll have the opportunity to meet Savassiea and my daughter Ayreonna. Congratulations Man. I'll see you when I get back."

"Congratulations to you too. Peace man."

Jackson hung up smiling at the events that had taken place. Just moments ago he was wondering what was in store for him as far as his life was concerned. And now he was about to start preparing for a wedding. He was ready to call Tate Robinson, the investment broker. He told him he'd call him sometime today with his decision of allowing him the opportunity to help him start his own business. He was definitely ready. He had prepared his resignation letter to Mr. Woodson weeks ago just in case. He felt good and was prepared for whatever life had for him.

It was ironic how things had changed right before him. And to think his friend kept a secret of having a daughter really threw him for a loop. He finished getting dressed and viewed himself in front of the two long gold mirrors on his closet doors. He smiled at the reflection for he was a change man and he was proud of what he was becoming and the challenges he was about to face. He was growing each and everyday for the better.

His spirit was in sync with where his heart and mind were directing, which was the road to peace and happiness and he couldn't help but smile back at the man he had become.

33
I'll Never Say Good-bye

Stacie wiped her face with the back of her leather glove as the small snowflakes kissed her face. She stood outside her home waiting for the limo to pick her up and to take her and the others to the Calvary United Methodist Church, where Michelle's funeral would be held. As she stood there, she thought about the fun she and Michelle shared together. She was really going to miss her. She was a good friend to her and she was glad God had brought them together no matter how short the moment was.

She cried as she reminisced about the conversation they all had with Michael. He told them about how he had met Michelle, although Stacie knew of the story she never disclosed it to the others for she felt it was something Michelle confided in her with. Michael was so distraught over Michelle's death he needed to talk to them about Michelle and how he loved her. His conversation enabled them to now understand why Michelle never mentioned him to them. She knew he was married and she never wanted to have a relationship with anyone who was still in that type of situation. Stacie respected her for that. It was hard for him losing Michelle at a time in his life when he was about to ask her to marry him. Stacie felt sorry for him as well as the others. He told them he had confessed his love and explained everything to Michelle as she was in a coma. He only hoped that she knew he really loved her and that he was going to do everything in his power to please her and make her happy.

Her thoughts were dismissed when she heard the car horn blowing. She could feel her heart sink as she walked towards the limo. Today was the day they all said good-bye to their beloved Michelle. And though she felt like breaking, she couldn't. She had to be strong for the others.

The driver opened the door for her and she slid in. She looked at Donna, Nicole and Michael and asked why this happened. They all hugged and cried a little while riding to the church.

Donna looked out the window. "Hey, look there's a rainbow! Who would have thought we'd see a rainbow in the middle of snowfall?" she exclaimed.

"I think it's a sign from Michelle, letting us know she is still with us as she always will be," Nicole stated. Stacie touched her hand and smiled.

Donna looked at her sister, reached over and hugged her. She knew how hard this was for her. "Hey let's pray," Donna announced. "It always helps me and we want the strength to carry on, right?"

"Right," Stacie said.

They all held hands as Donna began to pray. "Dear Father in Heaven, we know our Michelle is with you and we know it is best. For it is your will. God we thank you for allowing us the privilege of having Michelle as our friend. We thank you for allowing her to hear all the things each of us had to say to her in our own personal way. We thank you father for bringing her mother and father to her and allowing Michelle to know they still loved her. God we just ask for the strength to be strong during this time of departure. Be with us Lord. Comfort and protect us and reassure us that Michelle is not gone forever, but for just a moment. For we will rejoice with her in your mighty kingdom. Therefore, father we will not say goodbye, but see you soon. In the name of Jesus, Amen.

They all squeezed hands. "That was really beautiful Donna!" Michael said. They all knew they were going to be okay.

Upon arrival at the church, Stacie watched as Michelle's mother and father were led into the church. They wanted to stay at their daughter's place, despite Stacie's efforts of trying to get them to stay with her. They wanted to gather some of Michelle's things. And for some reason they felt that was where they should be and where they needed to be. And later the reason was very clear for them staying there.

Barbara awoke in the early morning hour. She made herself a hot cup of tea to help ease her mind and just to relax. She sat in the living room so that she wouldn't disturb her husband. She glanced at the pretty hope chest sitting in the far corner of the room. She opened it. She picked up a pretty gold book and realized that it was Michelle's journal.

She carried the small book back over to where she was sitting. Realizing what she was reading she closed the book. Moments later she opened it again. There were many things Michelle disclosed in her journal, however, Barbara's attention was focused on the last entry before the shooting.

October 8, 1996
Dear Journal,
A lot has happened today. But I feel good considering. I had been thinking of my Mother and Father today, wondering how they are. I will always love them, even though I feel as though my mother truly hates me. But I know now why she feels as she does. I would love to talk to her about her feelings. I know she was raped by my father, who was a white man.

Barbara placed her hands to her mouth and her teacup crashed to the floor. "Oh my God! She knew. But how?" she whispered.

I found my father with the help of Stacie. We did our own investigation (Stacie is very good too). Anyway, I found out his name is George Speer and he's in prison now for raping two other woman. He must be a really sick man. I confronted him. I went to prison and confronted him and I feel so much better. He cried when he met me of course telling me he didn't rape my mother. He wanted to be a part of my life, but his family would never accept me. But, I have proof that he raped my mother. For the first time I really felt what it was like to really hate someone. I hated him for hurting my mother and causing my mother to hate me. But because I'm in therapy, I'm able to try and deal with my emotions and feelings for both my mother and biological father. I am very ashamed of what I did to my stepfather. I have to apologize to him and my mother for the lie I told about him molesting me. I understand I was jealous of him for having the love from my mother that I so desperately wanted. But, through my sessions I'm learning to love me and not depend on another person's love. I only hope one day my mother can accept me as her daughter. I love both my mom and dad (step dad) so much.

Today Stacie went to an adoption agency to try and adopt a baby girl. I wonder why she doesn't just have her own. I guess it's because she's not married. I don't know! She should know December 2nd whether or not her paperwork went through. She's already met her little girl. She's 3 months old. I wonder what she'll name her if and when she gets her. I saw her too. She is so beautiful. Stacie will make an excellent mother. I wonder if I would.
Well that's it for now talk to you tomorrow.
M.

Barbara closed the book as her husband stood watching her. He sat beside her and rocked her in his arms. "It's going to be okay," he told her as he kissed her gently on her forehead.

It was a small private funeral with family and very close friends. David held Donna whenever he thought she was about to cry, which she did quit often. Everyone got up and spoke about Michelle, but it was when Michelle's Mother got up to speak that caused many tears to flow including Mrs. Garrett.

Michelle looked beautiful in her favorite color, blue. She looked to be peacefully sleeping. She was very beautiful and she was going to be missed by all who knew her.

In But A Moment

Stacie, Nicole, Donna and Michael, each placed a white rose in her coffin and kissed her tenderly on her forehead. Nicole stood looking down at Michelle, crying softly over her body. She knew she was going to miss her already. Stacie held her gently and told her Michelle was at peace now.

After the funeral everyone went back to Stacie's place for socializing and eating. Michael was scheduled to leave tomorrow morning as well as the Garretts. It was nice for everyone to get together and talk and share in the memories of Michelle. She would be missed but not forgotten.

Stacie portrayed the prefect hostess, talking with everyone and making sure everyone was okay. She managed to turn her focus to the faint ringing of the phone.

"Hello," she said in a pleasant tone.

"Hello, Miss Patterson?"

"This is she."

"This is Triple Rivers Adoption Agency."

Stacie's heart immediately began to pound. With all the confusion of the day she forgot it was December 2nd, the day for her to find out if her papers were approved for the adoption of the three-month-old little girl. The investigation took more than six months. And while it was going on she had to tell someone about what she had done. The only person she could think of was Michelle. She made Michelle promise not to tell. She didn't want the others to be disappointed if it fell through. Although she had told Michelle about her plans of adopting she never disclosed her medical situation to her.

"Oh hi," she said trying to sound calm. Are you calling about my paper work?"

"Yes, as a matter of fact Miss Patterson, I'm calling to let you know you can pick your daughter up tomorrow if you'd like." The woman had a big smile on her face.

"What? Do you mean I have a baby daughter?" Stacie felt the tears welled in her eyes. For once in her life she was no longer in control. "Oh my God!" she screamed.

Everyone came dashing into the sitting room, watching as Stacie sat on the floor crying.

"Stac, what's wrong?" Donna asked.

Stacie looked up at her friends. "I'm going to have a baby."

Donna looked puzzled. "Stacie what are you talking about?"

She laughed out loud. "I'm sorry Donna. I mean my adoption went through! I'm adopting a three-month-old baby girl, Donna. Can you believe it? I'm a mother!" she said smiling and crying at the same time. She immediately thought of Manzi when she announced she was going to be a mother. She wished she were still alive to share in her good news. But she knew she was sharing in it right now. Just as Michelle was.

They all ran over to her and hugged her.

"Well, now whose going to be the God-mother?" Nicole asked.

"I don't know I never even thought about that one."

Mrs. Garrett looked at her, knowing her daughter played a role in Stacie's adoption. She was proud and happy that Stacie's dream of adopting came true.

Everyone was so excited that it brought the saddened demeanor away. Now there were smiles and tears of joy. And Stacie knew in her heart, it was Michelle looking down and smiling.

"What's her name?" Michael asked

"Aubree Michelle Patterson." She smiled as she said her daughter's name.

"I love it, Stacie!" Donna told her as Nicole and Michael agreed. Stacie went over to Mrs. Garrett and hugged her as Mrs. Garrett thanked her.

"Michelle was so lucky to have you all in her life."

In But A Moment

"No, Mrs. Garrett we're the lucky ones. Michelle was a great person, whether you know it or not you've raised a great daughter. You should be proud."

"I wish I could have been there for Michelle when she truly needed me." she said sobbing

"She knows Mrs. Garrett, just like she knew I was going to adopt my little girl. Just like I know she'll never say good-bye and neither will we."

34
When you least expected it

Nicole agreed to drive Michael and the Garretts to the Airport. She felt as though she knew each of them all her life. And she felt better after talking with them on the ride to the Airport. Each of them agreed to stay in touch and visit at least once a year. She really liked Michael. He was a nice person and was soon to become a good friend to her. She was glad Michelle at least got to know how he really felt about her.

She realized how important friendship really was. It was great to know there were more important things in life then just having a man or being in a relationship. The past several months had helped her to grow in so many ways. She now saw how precious life really was and how important it was to love those who are a part of your life. For it was proved that so much could and would change in but a moment. She was grateful she had the opportunity to be a part of Michelle's life and to finally meet her parents and the man who loved her.   She thought about the miracle Stacie was about to receive and she couldn't wait to get home to see her new niece. She knew Stacie would consider her and Donna to be Aubree's aunts. She couldn't wait to spoil her. She had decided she was not going to take life for granted anymore. She was going to enjoy all that life had to offer. The first thing she wanted to do was travel. She made a mental note to touch base with her travel agent to see where a nice place would be to visit next summer. She was excited and feeling good.

She hugged the Garretts and Michael as their flight numbers were being called.

"Remember now, we said we keep in touch!" she told them.

In But A Moment

"You bet," Mr. Garrett said as he hugged her tight. He was glad his daughter had such good friends in her life. It was a blessing knowing that she had felt love throughout her life. He glanced over at his wife, he was even more blessed knowing that she had the opportunity to tell her daughter that she loved her.

He was glad he shared in the emotion. He smiled when he looked at Nicole, for it only made him think of good thoughts for his daughter. It was awesome to know that his daughter was truly loved and turned out to be a success despite her unfortunate circumstances with her mother. Looking at Nicole confirmed all of what he had hope for her.

Barbara Jean was going to do things differently. She was going to build something she never had with her own daughter, a bond of strength and love. It was all she could do in remembrance of her daughter.

After everyone had said their final good-byes and all the hugs and kisses had diminished, Nicole walked away with a feeling of sorrow and happiness. However, her ambition was to create an avenue of complete joy for all involved. She headed towards her car with a cheerful heart. She dug deep in her purse searching for her car keys.

"Now, I know I put those keys in here, where are they?" she said. The loud crash immediately jolted her thoughts as she looked towards the parking lot. "Darn! I knew this day was too good to be true," she shouted out loud unaware of the people staring at her. She ran over to the parking lot and saw a silver car. She threw her hands in the air. And as a tall, very attractive man exited the car, Nicole really didn't pay much attention.

"Excuse me Miss, is this your car?"

"Yes, I can't believe this has just happened." From the looks of the damage she knew it was going to cost.

"I'm really sorry. I will take care of the damage, if you agree we don't take this through our Insurance companies.

189

I've already accumulated enough accidents, thanks to my 17 year old son," he told her smiling.

"Well, I don't mind if you don't mind. But I think it may be a little expensive," she said continuing to look at the rear end of her car.

"No, I really don't mind. Considering the fact that if I get one more premium raise I'll be paying the cost of a car note instead of a premium," he stated.

"Oh, but there is a problem, I won't have a car to drive doing it your way. If I go through my Insurance at least I can get a rental car."

"I'd like to take care of that too, if you don't mind. In fact they have a rental place right here. I'll walk you over and give them the necessary information for you to leave with the car today. I'll call to have your car towed and taken to my mechanics today. It shouldn't take more than a couple of days for you to get your car back." He watched her hoping she would agree with the arrangements. He really couldn't afford any more conflict regarding his insurance.

Nicole watched him as he held his breath. "Okay, it's your dollar," she told him.

"If you got it like that, it's no problem with me." He extended his hand to her.

He breathed a sigh of relief. "Thank you. It's no problem I'll take care of everything. Shall we go and get that rental car now?" he asked.

"Sure," she replied.

They walked over towards the Rental Car office.

"I'm sorry at least I could introduce myself since I did cause an inconvenience for you."

Nicole smiled and she wondered who he was, that he was able to fork out so much money. She was very curious to learn more about him.

"I'm Craig Holiday." He held his hand out. He found her to be very attractive and interesting.

In But A Moment

Nicole greeted him. "Hello, I'm Nicole Grant. I guess I can't actually say it's a pleasure to meet you considering the fact that you caused such an unpleasant situation."

"Oh, but I'm trying to make up for it." He liked her and she had a great sense of humor. Though he was a prominent lawyer in Pittsburgh, he could have thought of other ways to spend his money. But for him it was okay spending it on her. He was almost glad he had literally run into her or at least her car.

"Yes, you're right it's very generous of you to take care of my expenses, that you caused." She was smiling and watching him.

"Is that sarcasm I hear?"

"No, not at all, just fact."

"Okay, really I want to thank you for allowing me to do this. It really does help me out," he told her.

"Well hey, maybe next time I can get a brand new car out of it. There's a new car lot just down the street," she said teasingly.

"Okay, okay, don't push your luck."

He had a gentle way about him and his eyes were kind and warm. She liked him immediately. Then she thought, is this fate? Or is this just some kooky case of insurance fraud. She had to find out a little more about him before she could determine what his intentions really were. "So, I'll bet your wife never allows your son to have the car, huh?

"Actually my wife died two years ago."

"Oh, I'm sorry," she said gingerly.

"Thanks. It's just me and my son. And I must admit I'm pretty lenient with him. We do have a great relationship. However, I do feel that maybe it's time he had his own car to bang around." He looked at her as she raised her eyebrows. "Just kidding, really he's only been in three accidents this year."

"Well don't you think that's pretty dangerous?"

191

"Well, yes, but they have only been mild accidents and believe it or not they were not his fault. All three times he was parked, and folks ran into him. He's really a great driver. He's had his license for a whole year now. And I told him I would help him to get his own car next year. He'll be going to college next year anyway and he works with me in the evenings and during summer. He's a pretty good kid and I'm proud of him."

"Well, thank God he didn't get his driving skills from his Dad!"

"Oh so we are sarcastic?" he asked moving closer towards her.

She just smiled. She didn't want to sound too anxious with her next question. She didn't want him to get the wrong impression. But she asked anyway.

"What type of work do you do Mr. Holiday?"

"I'm a lawyer and Mr. Holiday is what my clients call me." He touched her gently on her shoulder. "Please call me Craig."

"Okay, Craig."

A young woman walked over toward Craig and Nicole.

"Okay, Miss Grant, the attendant will bring your car around the front. Thank you." She handed Nicole the papers.

"Thank you," she said.

"Nicole how will I get in touch with you to let you know your car is ready?" he asked, hoping he didn't sound too frivolous.

She smiled at him and handed him a business card. He looked at the card and saw it only had her business phone number on it. He was hoping he could have her home number, but he didn't want to press it. And as though she was reading his mind, she removed the card from his hand and turned it over and placed her home number on the back. She handed the card to him and told him thank you for getting her car fixed and for allowing her to have a rental car until hers was finished.

In But A Moment

She headed to the car as he followed her. The attendant exited the car and held the door open for her.

"Thanks again," she said while entering the vehicle.

"Thank you," he whispered. "Thank you very much!"
He watched her as she drove away. He kissed the back of the card she had given him and placed it in the inside of his jacket pocket. He wanted to know her more all ready and he intended on doing just that.

35
What is Love?

Nicole told Donna all about her meeting with Craig Holiday. Donna knew Nicole liked him the minute she saw him, though she wouldn't admit it. She was happy for her. She knew her sister dated many different guys, but she never heard her sound so excited as she did talking about Craig. And she hadn't even gone on a date yet.

"So did you give him your home number?" Donna asked smiling at her sister.

"Well at first I didn't, but he was so persistent I gave in and gave it to him," she replied laughing as she hit her sister on the leg. "No, it really impressed me that he took care of the problem with my car and it was very generous of him to handle everything. Oh yeah, he's fine!" she told her cracking up laughing.

"Girl you are so crazy! Did you get his number?" "No, I didn't think to ask. Anyway he has to call because he has to let me know when my car is ready to be picked up."

"Well he could just have the auto body shop call to tell you that," she told her teasingly.

"Oh no he won't! He will call. I could tell he was more than interested." The ringing of the phone interrupted her.

"Oh maybe that's Mr. Holiday now," Donna told her. "No I doubt it, he probably doesn't know I've made it home yet. Besides I was driving so fast. I couldn't wait to get home to tell you what happened. So I know it's not him." She picked up the phone. "Hello?"

A deep sexy voice asked for her. "Hello, may I speak with Nicole please?"

"This is she," she said wondering who the mysterious voice belonged to.

In But A Moment

Donna watched her sister laughing and covering her mouth. "Is that him?" she whispered. Nicole gestured her hands to tell her to be quiet. She covered the phone with the palm of her hand. "No, I don't think it is!" she whispered to her sister.

"Well hello. This is Craig Holiday."

Nicole waved her hand towards her sister. "It's him!" she said as she moved closer and smiled.

"Oh hi Craig." She tried to sound nonchalant. "How are you?"

"Oh I'm fine. Listen the reason I'm calling. I hope you don't mind me calling. I'm aware you gave your home phone number for our car business, but I just thought maybe if you weren't doing anything this evening I could take you out to dinner as a token of my appreciation. May I?"

"Yes, you may. I'd like that." She knew she should have played a little hard to get but she liked him and she really did want to get to know him better.

"Great, I'll just need directions to your home. And I'll make reservations 7:00 PM. You do like steak?"

"Yes! As a matter of fact I love steak. Craig, I thought you couldn't drive your car? I assumed yours needed work too."

"It does. I just dropped it off at the auto shop where I had the tow truck take yours. However, I do have another car, although it's not as roomy."

She smiled at his comment. "Thanks. I'm going to give the phone to my sister."

Donna looked surprise and whispered. "For what?"

Nicole ignored her comment. "She gives better directions than me. You're coming from Church Hill, right?"

"Yes."

Donna got on the line and gave the directions. "It was nice talking to you Craig. I hope the directions are good for you. I look forward to meeting you." She handed the phone back to her sister.

"Your sister sounds nice Nicole I look forward to meeting her too. I'll see you at around 6:30 okay?"

"I am waiting." She hung up, "Well what do you think after talking to him?"

"He has a sexy voice. And he's a gentleman. You go girl!" she told her. "Have fun. Nicole, are you going to be afraid to eat in front of him? You know how we are, especially if it's someone you really like."

"I know I wondered about that, we'll see. I've got to go it's 4:00 PM and I need to look fabulous."

Donna watched her as she ran off. She was glad she found someone she really liked. Usually Nicole was always with someone she would just settle with and she was the one constantly giving. This time Donna could feel in her heart her sister had met someone who was going to treat her the way she deserved to be treated. She hadn't seen her sister smile this way for quite sometime. And for once she wasn't talking about love. She had a different persona when she spoke of Craig. Donna couldn't wait to meet him. This time Nicole was going on a real date. Someone who was going to hold her chair, take her coat and listen as she went on rambling about everything. She was going out with a gentleman, a man who knew what it was to treat a lady like a lady. She was going to take it slow. Besides what was love anyway? Love was a friend, someone who knew you inside outside. A confidant, someone who knew how to be affectionate, adoring, and spiritual. Love was her. And she was complete with herself now. And besides it was somebody else's lost if they decided to pass her by. Love she never expected it and there it was looking right at her and welcoming her to open arms.

36
<u>No Other Time Like This</u>

Donna finished the final touches for the Annual
Christmas Eve Party. This time they decided to have a
semi formal event. They had gone way out this year,
buying personalize favors for each of their guest. They were
having all the food catered this year. She was very excited
about this year's party. She wanted it to be perfect. Usually
children were not invited to their party, but this year there was
an exception. Everyone wanted to see Stacie's new baby. She
was going to bring her. Donna wanted a festive affair, to
break the sad mood that may be accompanied by them for not
having Michelle present.

Though she was there in spirit. It was not the same as
having her in person. So she made sure she framed the picture
she had of her, Michelle, Nicole and Stacie. She had it blown
up and placed it on the large wall opposite of the tree.

Donna stood in front of the large picture window and
smiled as the tiny crystal like snowflakes fell. It was a
beautiful picture of snow tipped trees with the beautiful tiny
lights sparkling. She thought of all that had taken place within
the year and tears fell from her eyes. So many miracles had
happened in just a short amount of time. She knew there
would never be another moment like the one she was in right
now. She was finally able to see her sister have a true love,
someone who truly loved her and cherished her. She was glad
Craig and Nicole met, she liked him the minute she met him.
They made a handsome couple. She had never known Nicole
to spend so much time with one man before. She was happy
and that made Donna happy to see her smiling as she did.

She thought of her friends. Each of them. Stacie,
adopting Aubree, her dream. Carmella and Jackson getting
married and Carmella being able to encourage Darletta into
getting help for her pain. They were sisters again and Darletta

was coping with the HIV and doing well now that she got the medical attention she needed.

"Thank you God," she said.

And Michelle making it into Heaven and shining down on them. And for her being able to make peace with her parents. "What a powerful blessing God left us with", she whispered. "You are so good, so awesome." And lastly she thanked God for David, the joy of her life. And then she cried tears of joys for all her blessings. Oh how thankful she was to be a child of God and to know him for herself.

She went to the bathroom and freshened up.

"Donna, there you go slow as ever. Everyone will be here in about 30 minutes."

"I know," she told her sister. "I just want to freshen up a little."

She was wearing a beautiful form fitting long black backless dress with gold jewels hanging from the bottom of the dress. She looked beautiful. Nicole wore an emerald green form fitting dress cut low in the front with tiny white pearls absorbing the mesh material. She wore her hair pulled high on top of her head. She looked exquisite.

Nicole smiled at her sister when she finally came out of the bathroom. She walked over to her and told her how beautiful she looked.

"Are you trying to get sentimental on me Nicole?"

"No, not really. I just think you really look pretty that's all."

She was sentimental, because this was more than their annual Christmas Eve party. Something grand was going to happen this evening and she was glad she was a part of it. She loved her very much.

"Oh I was just wondering, because usually I'm the one always about ready to cry," she told her sister as she reached to hug her.

"Donna can you do me a favor?"

"Sure, what is it?"

"I forgot one important thing. Don't be made at me. I know I'll never be as organized as you."

"What is it?"

She looked at her sister trying to look pitiful. "I forgot to pick up the favors were giving out this evening." She shut her eyes for fear of Donna's impression. She knew she had purposely forgot to pick the favors up. She needed some type of excuse to get Donna to leave the house.

"Ah Nicole! I could just kill you."

"I know, I would go myself, but I promised Stacie I'd pick her and Aubree up since her car is in the shop." She wanted to laugh so bad when she saw the look on her sister's face. Everyone should be on their way including Stacie. She knew Stacie's car wasn't in the shop, but she couldn't think of anything else to tell her.

"Okay," Donna told her. I'll go, it may take me a little while to get back though since, thanks to you I have to drive to Monroeville."

"Okay great! Hopefully not everyone will be on time. You know how that goes. But I promise I won't start anything without you."

"Okay, I'll see you in a bit." She went out the door.

Nicole ran to the window to make sure she was in the car and off. Exactly 15 minutes later the guests started to arrive. Oreon was first to arriv. Carmella and Jackson and Darletta were shortly behind him, while another couple entered with them. Nicole wasn't sure she recognized them. Carmella introduced Bill and Savassiea. Nicole greeted them. She hugged Carmella and Carmella introduced her to Jackson too. Nicole was not sure what to say to Darletta. Darletta hugged her and told her how beautiful everything looked. It shock Nicole how pleasant she was. Donna had told her everything as far as Darletta, Carmella and Jackson. Therapy must do wonders she thought to herself. Next, Nicole and Donna's parents entered. So did David's mother. She hugged and greeted them.

"You didn't give anything away, now did you sweetheart?" her dad asked.

"No daddy, of course not. Although this was the hardest secret in the world to keep from her."

"I know, that's why I want to make sure you didn't say anything. I know how close you two are."

By that time Stacie and the baby arrived. Everyone ran over to her to get a peep at Aubree. She was truly a beautiful baby. Stacie dressed her up for the occasion. She wore a little white dress with white fur on the collar and sleeve. Something everyone knew Nicole had bought. She was a little doll baby.

"Ah look at Doll!" It was a nickname they adopted from Michelle. She was always calling someone doll. They thought it would be appropriate for Aubree.

David entered the house while everyone was gathered around Stacie and the baby.

"Hey, y'all, what's up?" he announced, trying to get everyone's attention. Finally Jackson and Bill came over and greeted him. After a few minutes David's mother and the Grant's as well as Nicole came over and hugged up.

"Are you nervous David?" Nicole asked him smiling.

"Actually I'm not as nervous as I thought I'd be."

It was a small world. David had known Jackson for over three years. He had worked on an engineering project with him through his company. He had also met Bill through Jackson. He never knew Carmella was engaged to Jackson. He liked her immediately. She seemed very sweet. He couldn't believe it when Bill told him he had gotten married. He knew the kind of lifestyle Bill lead and he was glad he found someone to settle down with. They joked about their getting hitched. Soon Craig arrived. Nicole hugged and kissed him tenderly on the lips.

"Look at you, you are absolutely gorgeous." He hugged her again.

In But A Moment

"Well I must say, you look grand yourself." She reached up and kissed him again. Stacie ran over to meet Mr. Right. She later told Nicole how handsome he was and how she could tell he cherished her.

"I'm very happy for you sweetie." She hugged and kissed her on the cheek.

"Thanks Stace."

"I guess your ship finally came in, we won't be needing to take that cruise now."

"Who says?" she asked smiling at her friend.

She had never been happier than what she was at that very moment. All the people she loved were there ready to celebrate with her. Life was okay, she thought tenderly. She walked over towards the window and glanced out as the tiny snowflakes kissed the ground. She felt someone hug her from behind. It was Craig. She turned around and hugged him.

"You look blissful," he said while holding her.

"I am honey, I am. I waited for so long to find someone to share my life with. I've played so many games with men that didn't mean me any good and then here you come when I least expect it, loving me like nobody's business. And now I'm standing in my place looking at all the people I love ready to share something. So if I look blissful to you, it's because I truly am. Thank you."

"For what, baby?"

"For rescuing me at just the right time."

"Best moment of my life," he told her.

"I'm so glad you're happy, baby. But I just want you to know, you ain't seen nothing yet." She smiled up at him and kissed him.

The doorbell rang and startled her, as everyone got quiet. Donna does have her key?" Nicole's mother asked.

"Yes she does. I have no idea who that could be." She walked over to the front and opened it. She screamed when she saw who was standing there. Everyone ran over to the doorway to see who it was.

"Michael and Mr. and Mrs. Garrett! I can't believe you guys are here. It seems as though I just left you guys," she cried as she hugged them. She grabbed onto to their arms and pulled them inside. She introduced them to everyone. The night was so perfect for them. This would be the best Christmas ever she thought as she watched everyone mingling, laughing. She could feel the true meaning of Christmas and it touched her soul. She glanced at the clock and figured Donna should be back any minute. She asked to have everyone's attention.

"Donna should be here any minute guys."

And just as she said it she heard Donna's car. "Okay, everyone, she's here."

Donna got out of the car and smiled when she saw all the cars. She looked up at the windows and saw how beautiful everything looked. She stopped for a moment and thanked God for giving them such a beautiful night to have their party. She felt butterflies and couldn't figure out why. She reached the door and noticed that all she saw were Christmas lights and the lights from the tree. She found that to be odd. She at least expected the kitchen light to be turned on. She turned the knob and entered.

"Surprise!" yelled everyone.

She looked puzzled. "Surprise? What are y'all talking about surprise?" And as she said it David moved forward. The only thing that was heard was soulful Christmas music. She watched David as everyone in the place looked on. Nicole was already crying and so were Stacie and Mrs. Grant. Donna slowly looked around the room. She had spotted Michael and the Garretts. It brought tears to her eyes when she saw them. David moved closer to her and kissed her tenderly on the lips.

She was crying now.

"David."

He placed his fingers on her lips. "Here baby." He handed her a white box. She gasped when she opened the

202

box. There stood perfectly the 14KT gold tiger carrying a black sack on his back with her baby cub peeking out of the sack. The statue fit perfectly in her hand. She knew how expensive it was. It was the tiger she saw in the shop at the airport. How could he know about that tiger? Then she looked at her sister, who was crying and she smiled at her. The tiger had emerald jewels for the eyes.

"Thank you baby, it's so beautiful." She couldn't stop crying. He looked at her. She was so beautiful and he truly loved her with all of his heart.

"I'm glad you like it baby."

"I love it," she whispered as she hugged him tightly.

"Baby, did you know that little cub comes out?"

"Ah, no I didn't know that." She slowly lifted the little cub from its sack and as she removed it a 2-carat diamond ring attached to his paw peered out at her.

"Oh my God, David, Oh my God!"

"Will you marry me?"

"Oh baby, why yes, of course I will! I love you David Johnson, I love you so much!" she cried as tears streamed down her face.

Everyone congratulated her as they viewed the beautiful ring. She went to her mother and father as she walked towards them holding Nicole's hand. Her mother cried, for she knew how happy both her daughters were. And she was so proud of them. They were good children.

"Honey?" She touched both her daughter's cheeks. "Daddy and I are so proud of you two. You two are truly a blessing to us. Be happy!"

They hugged each other and the tears flowed. And as everyone got back into the festive mood of the holiday spirit, Donna entered her bedroom and shut the door. And she looked up to the ceiling as the tears stained her cheeks. "You are truly, truly awesome! Thank you for my Blessings!"